'Miss Manning, have *you* met the great hero of the day?' Lady Alnworth said.

He turned to smile at Mary, and it took all her long years of careful diplomatic training to keep her own polite smile in place. A chivalric knight of old, only in a red coat instead of gleaming armour. On him, that uniform seemed—different. Exotic. Alluring.

'How do you do, Miss Manning?' he said, bowing over her hand.

His breath through her glove made her shiver. His hair was a golden brown, shimmering as if he spent much time in the sun. It gave him such a warmth she wanted to get close to. So very vital…burning with raw, energetic *life*.

Yes, she thought. No wonder all the young ladies of London were in love with him. If she wasn't careful she would soon be one of them!

Author Note

I don't know what last winter was like where you are, but here it was cold, grey and long! I am *not* a winter person—ever… So I definitely loved escaping to the warm beaches of Brazil, even if it was only in my imagination.

I also loved watching the romance of Mary and Sebastian unfold against the palm trees and real-life political intrigue of 1808 Rio. They started to feel like real friends—two people whose adventures I loved following every day. I was never sure where they would go, but I knew they definitely belonged together—two strong, kind-hearted, brave people, who are too honourable and stubborn for their own good! Maybe I was just feeling extra-romantic after my own wedding last summer! I hope you enjoy their adventures, too…

For more behind-the-book history and deleted scenes from *The Demure Miss Manning* be sure to visit me at ammandamccabe.com.

THE DEMURE
MISS MANNING

Amanda McCabe

Published in Great Britain 2015
by Mills & Boon, an imprint of Harlequin (UK) Limited,
Eton House, 18-24 Paradise Road, Richmond, Surrey, TW9 1SR

© 2015 Ammanda McCabe

ISBN: 978-0-263-24815-9

Harlequin (UK) Limited's policy is to use papers that are natural, renewable and recyclable products and made from wood grown in sustainable forests. The logging and manufacturing processes conform to the legal environmental regulations of the country of origin.

Printed and bound in Spain
by CPI, Barcelona

Amanda McCabe wrote her first romance at the age of sixteen—a vast epic, starring all her friends as the characters, written secretly during algebra class. She's never since used algebra, but her books have been nominated for many awards, including the RITA, Romantic Times Reviewers' Choice Award, the Booksellers' Best, the National Readers' Choice Award, and the Holt Medallion. She lives in Oklahoma with her husband, one dog and one cat.

Books by Amanda McCabe

Mills & Boon Historical Romance and Mills & Boon Historical *Undone!* eBooks

Bancrofts of Barton Park

The Runaway Countess
Running from Scandal
Running into Temptation (Undone!)

Linked by Character

A Notorious Woman
A Sinful Alliance
High Seas Stowaway
Shipwrecked and Seduced (Undone!)

Stand-Alone Novels

Betrayed by His Kiss
The Demure Miss Manning

More Mills & Boon Historical *Undone!* eBooks by Amanda McCabe

To Court, Capture and Conquer
Girl in the Beaded Mask
Unlacing the Lady in Waiting
One Wicked Christmas
An Improper Duchess
A Very Tudor Christmas

Visit the Author Profile page at millsandboon.co.uk for more titles.

Chapter One

❦

'I hear he is the handsomest thing ever seen!'

Mary Manning tried not to laugh at her friend Lady Louisa Smythe's enthusiastic words. Instead, she smiled and nodded at the people they strolled past in the park, and adjusted her lace-trimmed parasol against the bright afternoon sun. Lady Louisa did tend to get so very excited over titbits of gossip, especially gossip about good-looking young men.

And a good-looking young man who was the newest hero of the war against Napoleon, after his valiant behaviour at the Battle of Caldiero—well, Mary was surprised she hadn't swooned quite away with enthusiasm yet.

But Mary had to admit even she was intrigued by the tales of Lord Sebastian Barrett, third son of the Marquess of Howard and a captain in the Third Hussars, and his heroism. Just a tiny bit.

Lady Louisa took Mary's arm as they turned along a winding, narrow river path. Mary automatically studied the people gathered there, strolling in pairs or laughing quartets, talking together by the sun-dappled water. Her father had worked in the diplomatic service for as long as she could remember, and she had been his hostess since her beautiful Portuguese mother died a few years ago.

Sixteen had been young to organise dinners and card parties where foreign envoys and their sophisticated wives could make alliances with the English representatives, especially in such dangerous wartime days, yet there had been no one else to do it. Mary had already learned much from watching her gracious mother, listening to her parents' conversations, asking questions. She loved the work, loved having a purpose. Loved learning new things. With her father, she had seen Italy and Austria, lived in Russia for many months, only returning to England a few months ago.

Yet sometimes—well, sometimes she almost wished she could giggle and whisper like other young ladies, be carried away by the wild wings of flirtation and infatuation. Just for a moment. That was why she so enjoyed being friends with Lady Louisa.

'The handsomest man *ever*?' Mary said. She and Lady Louisa stopped in the shade of a copse of trees where they could watch the crowds flow past, the children sailing their toy boats on the water, the bright flutter of beribboned bonnets and silk parasols. 'Better looking than the Prince de Ligne? You swore last week he had quite won your heart for ever.'

Louisa laughed merrily. 'Oh, him! He is to marry some little German dumpling of a duchess, trying to get his lands back. He was a fine dancer, to be sure, but he is no hero like Lord Sebastian. There is just something about a man in uniform, don't you think, Mary? A wonderful manly spirit.'

A naval officer in his blue coat and cocked hat strolled past just then, giving them a bow and a grin. Louisa giggled and fluttered her handkerchief at him.

Mary bit her lip to keep from smiling. It seemed *any* uniform would do, Army or Navy.

She thought of the stories she had heard of Lord Sebastian, how he fought off ten Frenchmen in hand-to-hand combat, had several horses shot from beneath him. She was sure they could not all be true, but she liked the tales anyway. Fairy stories had always appealed to her, ever since she was tiny and her mother would tell her Portuguese myths at bedtime. Ancient battles, knights, fair maidens.

Louisa leaned closer to whisper in Mary's ear. 'Though I am sure Lord Sebastian can be no more handsome than his brother Lord Henry. You should have no worries on *that* score.'

Mary looked at her friend, startled. How did Louisa know of Lord Henry and his vague sort of courtship? 'Lord Henry Barrett?'

Louisa's smile turned secretive. 'Why, yes. For is he not a great admirer of yours?'

Mary felt her cheeks turn warm and not from the touch of the sun beyond the edge of her parasol. She looked away, staring hard at a child with a wildly waving hoop dashing past with his nurse in pursuit. 'I wouldn't say that. We have only met once or twice.'

'No?' Louisa already seemed distracted by a gentleman on horseback in the distance. 'Are you quite sure? You two would surely be a most suited pair. My uncle says Lord Henry's future in the diplomatic service seems assured. That he might even be sent to Russia soon, like your father.'

A most suited pair. So they would be. Lord Henry Barrett had become something of a protégé to her father in recent days. Sir William Manning never complained of having only a daughter, only Mary, but she knew he would have liked a son to follow in his career footsteps, whom he could guide and advise amid the powder keg of politics and wars and royal courts.

Her father had asked her to invite Lord

Henry to some of their dinners lately, and often the two of them were talking afterward in the library for many hours. Much longer than Lord Henry had ever talked with Mary herself.

A promising young man indeed, Mary dearest, her father had said only that morning, as she prepared to go out walking with Louisa. *Steady and calm, exactly what this country needs now.*

Mary sighed as those words echoed in her mind. She twirled her parasol, thinking of Lord Henry Barrett. He was handsome enough, with golden hair and a careful, polite smile. The perfect diplomat, correct, poised, giving nothing away, barely even touching her hand in a dance.

A man somewhat like her father must have been, in fact, before he met her beautiful mother in Lisbon and brought her home to London. A man her father would surely like to see her matched with, so she could continue in what she was trained to do. To be a hostess and helpmate in foreign postings. A diplomat herself in all but title.

Mary knew that would be the best path in her life. The only path, really. All she knew.

Yes, Lord Henry Barrett would be a suitable match. Tales of his dashing, heroic Army brother were only that—thrilling fairy stories.

'Lord Henry is amiable,' Mary said carefully. 'But I don't know him well enough to say whether he admires me or not.'

'Really? I am sure he must. You would be the perfect diplomat's wife.' Louisa idly tapped her folded fan against her pink-striped skirts, watching the passers-by as if she searched for another handsome face. 'And he is the second son, after all, where Lord Sebastian is the third. He might succeed to an earldom one day.'

'Louisa,' Mary said with a laugh, 'of all Lord Henry's advantages, I would say that is most implausible. I have heard the wife of the eldest brother is expecting.'

'Oh.' Louisa gave a little pout. 'How disappointing. I should have so liked to be bosom bow with a countess. You shall have to make do with being Lady Henry, I suppose. And perhaps *I* shall be Lady Sebastian! We could be sisters!'

Mary laughed even more. That was why she liked being friends with Louisa. All the people who came to her father's house, as interesting as they were, were so very solemn. Louisa made her laugh. 'You have not even met Lord Sebastian yet, Louisa. How can you know if you would like him enough to marry him?'

'Because sometimes a lady just knows!' Louisa seized Mary's hand and pulled her along behind her back on to the pathway. 'He sounds handsome and brave and dashing. Exactly what I should be looking for, don't you think?'

Mary nodded. Were those not things *every* lady should look for? Except for sensible, useful ladies like herself, of course. She was supposed to look for someone she could help, a family she could fit into. Yet she couldn't quite help envisioning a tall, lean, darkly handsome figure at the head of a great cavalry charge. The stuff of epic poems.

Louisa tugged her out past the park gates, chattering about a pretty bonnet she had glimpsed in a window and 'quite coveted'. Carriages and fine horses clattered past in a great parade.

'I think we are very near Lady Alnworth's house,' Louisa said. 'We should call on her. She promised to lend me her amethyst bracelet to go with my lavender gown for the Seeton ball tomorrow night.'

Lady Alnworth was one of the greatest hostesses in London—and one of the most scandalous, at the centre of a dashing crowd. 'I am not so sure, Louisa. My father will be home soon and wanting his dinner.'

'It will only take a moment! Besides, you know that Lady Alnworth always has all the latest news. Perhaps she will know if Lord Sebastian will be at the ball tomorrow.'

Mary laughed. Perhaps Lady Alnworth was not the very most high-in-the-instep lady in town, but she was respectable enough. And news was always welcome. 'Very well. Just for a moment.'

They made their way to Lady Alnworth's house, a tall, bright-white structure at the edge of the park. As always, her doors were open to visitors and the clatter of talk and laughter flowed out into her lavishly decorated hall. It was a lively, fashionable, bright house and suddenly Mary was rather glad they had come.

'Is Lady Alnworth at home?' Louisa asked the butler.

'Indeed she is, Lady Louisa, Miss Manning,' he answered with a bow. 'A large party has just arrived before you, including the Duchess of Thwaite.'

Louisa's eyes widened and even Mary was rather impressed. The duchess seldom came to town, choosing to keep her own almost-constant house party at Thwaite Park. Whenever she graced a London party, she trailed clouds of illustrious friends behind her. She usually only came to town for her annual ball.

'The duchess is here?' Mary asked.

'Yes, with several guests, Miss Manning,' the butler answered, solemnly but with a twinkle in his eyes. '*Heroic* guests.'

'Heroic?' Louisa squealed. 'Oh, Mary! What if it is Lord Sebastian, and maybe some of his Army friends? How very exciting. I knew it was a good idea to call on Lady Alnworth today.'

'Louisa, surely it is not…' Mary began, but Louisa was already dashing off towards the half-open drawing-room doors.

By the time Mary caught up to her, following at the polite pace long years at royal courts with her parents and strict governesses had taught her, Louisa was already at the group gathered around the tall, open windows that looked out on to the park. Mary paused to study them, to gauge the scene, as she would a painting. As she had always been taught to do.

The duchess was at the centre of the group, tall and dark-haired, dressed in the height of fashion in a green-and-black pelisse and tall-crowned green hat, with Lady Alnworth lounging on a brocade *chaise* beside her in a red classical robe. They looked very dramatic with Louisa, all blonde curls and satin ribbons, fluttering to greet her. A tea table laden with a gleaming silver service was laid before them and they were surrounded by laughing admirers vying for their attention.

Mary felt suddenly shy. She had been taught

to be comfortable around different sorts of people, to talk to anyone in a polite fashion, but these people were more than polite—they were known as the wittiest group in London. She recognised Mr Nicholas Warren and Lord Paul Gilesworth, two of the most sought-after society bachelors, and Lord James Sackville, but not another man who stood half in the shadows of the window curtaining, looking out at the park.

'Miss Manning,' Lady Alnworth called. 'Won't you come in and help us settle a question? You are always so clever, so well read. Lord James here says Plato cannot be a pagan since he advocates the immortality of the soul, while Mr Warren claims that cannot be. I am terribly confused.'

'I fear my reading is not so extensive as all that, Lady Alnworth. I have only read what Plato reported Socrates, his teacher, to have said,' Mary said, making her way towards their hostess with her brightest smile. 'I know little about...'

She suddenly noticed a movement from the man near the window, a flutter of colour that caught her attention. A man in a red uniform coat stepped forward, into a buttery blade of sunlight, and Mary faltered at the sight of him.

He was quite, quite beautiful, almost unreal, like something in a book suddenly sprung into vivid life. A chivalric knight of old, only in a red coat instead of gleaming armour. On him, that uniform seemed—different. Exotic. Alluring.

He was taller than most of the men she met in London, with enticingly broad shoulders and lean hips, long hips encased in pale breeches set off with tall, glossy black boots.

His hair was a gold-tinged brown, almost tawny, shimmering as if he spent much time in the sun. It gave him such an enticing glow, a warmth, she feared she wanted to get closer and closer to, as if he could melt every tiny sliver of ice around her. Of the loneliness that had seemed to close in around her since her mother died. That hair fell in unruly waves over his brow and the high, gild-trimmed collar of his coat, enticingly soft-looking.

He didn't seem as if he really quite belonged in the gilded, brocaded drawing room, despite his immaculate uniform and a noble bearing. Mary imagined him on the deck of a pirate ship, riding through a stormy sea, or racing a wild horse madly across an open field.

Or maybe grabbing a sighing, melting lady up into his arms, kissing her passionately until she swooned.

Mary almost laughed aloud at her romantic fantasies. Obviously she was mistaken when she told Lady Alnworth that she hadn't read so widely; she had been consuming too many poems lately. It was very unlike her. If this was the famous Lord Sebastian Barrett, his reputation was more than justified. He was quite perfectly handsome.

She thought of Lord Henry Barrett, the man everyone seemed to think she should marry, who was perfectly amiable and good-looking, and felt a bit sorry for him.

'Lady Louisa, Miss Manning!' the duchess cried. 'I am so glad to see you both. Come, sit with us. You can assist us in this quarrel between Lord James and Mr Warren. But what we really want to do is get Lord Sebastian to tell us of his many adventures. Perhaps you shall have more luck.'

'Oh, yes, you must tell us more, Lord Sebastian!' Louisa cried. 'How heroic of you to defend us all like that.'

'Lady Louisa, I know you once met Lord Sebastian. Miss Manning, have *you* met the great hero of the day?' Lady Alnworth said. 'He has so long been away from London, sadly for us all. Much like yourself. Lord Sebastian Barrett, may I present Miss Mary Manning?'

He turned to smile at Mary and it took all her long years of careful diplomatic training to keep her own polite smile in place, to make him the regulation demure curtsy. Up close, his eyes were very, very green. As green as her mother's treasured emerald earrings, deep and dark, set in a lean, sculpted face touched with the gold of the sun. Even in all her family's travels, she had never met a man quite like this one before. So very vital, burning with raw, energetic *life*.

Yes, she thought wryly. No wonder all the young ladies of London were quite in love with him. If she wasn't careful, she would soon be one of them.

But one thing Mary had learned above all was to be careful.

'How do you do, Miss Manning,' he said, bowing over her hand. His breath felt so warm through her glove, but somehow it made her shiver. 'I believe I have heard of your father. Sir William Manning, the diplomat who was lately in St Petersburg?'

'Oh, yes, he is my father,' Mary said, feeling quite pleased he had heard of her family in some way. 'We've only been back in London for a few months. He is waiting for his next post.'

Lord Sebastian's handsome face looked very solemn suddenly, like a grey cloud sliding over the sun. 'My friend Mr Denny says he and his wife could never have escaped from France last year without Sir William's help. He could not say enough fine things about your father.'

Mary couldn't help but smile at hearing her father's praises. She well remembered the long nights he had gone sleepless while trying to help every British citizen he could. 'He would be pleased to hear that your friend is well now, but I know he would claim he only did his duty for England. As you do, Lord Sebastian. We do hear such talk of your heroics.'

An embarrassed look flashed across his handsome face and he glanced away. He laughed and it was as smooth and warm as his fine looks. 'I did nothing but laze around in the Spanish sun, I promise, Miss Manning. It's people like you and your father who are the heroes of our country, digging your way through Russian ice and snow to win friends for England.'

Mary had to laugh, too, charmed by how he seemed to want to run away from his heroic reputation rather than revel in it, as any other man surely would. 'It was indeed—interesting in Russia, Lord Sebastian. I am glad to be back in London now.'

'I should very much like to hear more about your experiences there, Miss Manning.'

'Would you truly?' Mary said, surprised. 'I promise it was really quite dull.'

'I always love hearing about other lands. My

favourite book as child was *Thousand and One Nights*. Do you know it?'

'Of course! It was my favourite, too,' Mary said. Lord Sebastian, despite his fine looks and great popularity, was not so frightening after all. It felt as though she already knew him, that she could tell him of some of her secret hopes. Her thirst for adventure. 'I fear I made my nanny read it to me over and over until she was quite sick of it.'

'What are you two talking of so intently?' Lady Alnworth called. 'You must share it with all of us, I insist!'

Mary glanced at their hostess, suddenly startled to realise she and Lord Sebastian had been standing beside the half-open window, talking quietly together for too long. It was most unlike her to lose sight of even a second of impropriety. She felt her cheeks turn warm and quickly smiled to cover her blushes.

Lady Alnworth and Louisa sat with two of the other men, Mr Warren and Lord Paul Gilesworth, two of the most well-known rakes in town. They all looked at her with eyes wide with interest.

'I fear I was the one monopolising Miss Manning,' Lord Sebastian said with a charming smile. 'I was asking about her time in Russia.'

'Oh, it must have been horrid, all that dreadful snow!' the duchess cried, with a quick agreement from Lady Alnworth. 'Surely there are far more amusing things going on right here in London.'

'Perhaps we could speak more about your travels later, Miss Manning?' Lord Sebastian whispered in her ear before she could move away.

He wanted to talk more to *her*? Mary could only nod, frozen with something terribly like excitement and—and pleasure. It was most frightening. He led her back to the group, and soon they were all deep in a conversation about the newest play at Covent Garden. But Mary was always much too aware of Lord Sebastian sitting across from her, of his warm laughter and emerald-green eyes. The way the duchess kept sliding her hand over his arm.

Mary knew she was going to have to be

very careful indeed. One careless step and her cautious, contented life could come tumbling down—right into those strong arms.

Chapter Two

'That Lady Louisa Smythe is a rare beauty,' Lord Paul Gilesworth said with a laugh. He gestured to the footman for a bottle of port as they settled into armchairs by the fireplace of their club in St James's, after leaving Lady Alnworth's tea. 'Also a rare flirt, it seems. What do you all think?'

Nicholas Warren laughed. 'I think her father guards her like a chest of gold. You'd have far better luck with Lady Alnworth herself, Gilesworth.'

'Do you think so?' Gilesworth said, his expression turning speculative. 'Depends on what you want the fillies for, I suppose. Brood mare or racehorse? And what of the Duchess of Thwaite? She would be a bit of a challenge.'

Sebastian watched as the servants poured out the blood-red wine into fine cut-crystal goblets, half-listening as his friends debated the merits of various ladies in London. He felt as he had ever since he returned to England—distant from everything that went on around him, as if it was happening in a dream.

The concerns of London society, the concerns that had once been his as well, seemed as insubstantial and inconsequential as the bubbles in a glass of champagne. The beauties of various débutantes, who had lost what in which card games, who took which famous actress as his mistress—it all meant nothing at all after what he had seen. What he had done in battle.

He took a long drink of the fine, satin-smooth wine, and studied the faces of his old friends, as detached as if he looked at paintings in a gallery. Nicholas Warren was all right; a kind-hearted, harmless sort of chap, headed for the diplomatic service like Sebastian's brother Henry. But Gilesworth and Lord James, who had seemed like such fun companions when they were at school, now had concerns that seemed no deeper than the cut of their coats and the legs of the dancing girls at Covent Garden. It was rather wearying.

Sebastian couldn't help but remember the men he had seen fall in battle. Good, brave men, who lived to the fullest, yet died fearlessly for their country. He had drunk with them, too, sat up late into the night joking and laughing, gone searching for beautiful women to seek comfort in their arms for a few moments. Faced the deepest instants of life and death with them.

Yet somehow, it had felt so very different with his fellow officers. Life had taken on a rare, shining edge there on the eve of battle. A height of feeling he had never known.

And now those friends were gone, and Sebastian felt as if he had plunged into a dark tunnel where there was no point of light to guide him. Much to his shock, he was hailed as a hero here in London. Welcomed warmly into every drawing room, begged for his 'stories'. Even his father, who had long bemoaned how 'useless' his youngest son was, such a wastrel, seemed proud.

It made Sebastian feel the greatest fraud and

he was puzzled that no one else seemed to see it. He was alive and all those good men were dead in the gore of the battlefield.

Surely there was nothing right about that?

But no one here seemed to understand anything. They went on blithely with their lives as if nothing else mattered. As if the world outside their little island wasn't exploding into pieces.

Sebastian no longer felt he belonged in London. No longer belonged in his own skin. Lord Sebastian Barrett—who was that? With his fellow officers, he had felt he found himself, his true self, at last. For so long, his whole life really, he had felt the tug between what he felt inside and what his family thought. Once he was in the Army, he could just—be. Here, there was only a cold numbness, that terrible distance. He found he would do anything, try anything, to be warm again.

The only time he had felt anything since he came home was when Miss Mary Manning had smiled up at him today in Lady Alnworth's drawing room. Miss Manning wasn't flashing and flirtatious like her friend Lady Louisa, to be sure, but there was such a quiet, dignified beauty to her. A solemn, deep perception in her grey eyes that he hadn't found in anyone else in London. They all swirled on with their merriment, never stopping to look.

Yet Mary Manning seemed to look. Her very stillness seemed to be a refuge, no matter how brief. He had wanted to sit with her, talk to her more. Maybe even tell her something of what had happened to him.

But he remembered all too well that his father had declared Miss Manning would be a suitable bride/for Sebastian's brother Henry. The perfect, intellectual son, destined to carry on the Barretts' great tradition in the diplomatic service. Sebastian had thought nothing of it when he heard his father and Henry talking about Mary Manning. After all, he did not know her and his thoughts and nightmares were still all of the battlefield. He didn't care who his brother married. Surely they would be the perfect, dignified couple, a credit to the Barretts and to England.

It was obvious Henry cared little for Miss Manning beyond who her father was, the famous and well-respected Sir William Manning. That was how all their family's marriages were conducted.

Yet now Sebastian had met Mary Manning. And she was most unexpected.

He took a deep drink of his wine, draining the glass. The footmen quickly refilled it. So, the brief moment of quiet Sebastian had found in Mary's pale grey eyes had been all too brief. The desperate search for distraction went on.

He studied the faces of his friends again, sweet Nicholas Warren and Lord James who would always follow him anywhere. But Paul Gilesworth—he always knew where the most trouble was to be found. He revelled in it. He would surely know of something that would make Sebastian forget the great waste of his life for a time.

'So, no Lady Louisa Smythe,' Gilesworth was saying with a laugh. It seemed Sebastian had missed more of the listing of various ladies' attributes. 'She would surely be easy enough to lead astray, but the trouble with her father afterward wouldn't be worth it. I for one have no intention of ending in parson's mouse-trap before I'm forty.'

'But that's the trouble with every young lady in London,' Lord James said with a sigh. 'Their papas are most vigilant.'

Gilesworth gave a sly laugh. 'Not all of them, surely.'

'For respectable young ladies, it must be,' Nicholas said earnestly. 'That is how it should be. But *demi-reps*…'

'Where is the challenge in that? Or even in flirtatious young misses like Lady Louisa,' Gilesworth said, his lips twisting.

A challenge. Surely that was what Sebastian needed now. He gestured for more wine as he turned that intriguing thought over in his head. Every day in the Army was a challenge. In London, there was only ever that numbness.

'What do you mean, Gilesworth?' Sebastian said. The others turned to him with startled looks on their faces, as if they had rather forgotten he was there. 'What of a challenge could there be in London?'

Gilesworth's eyes narrowed. He looked as if he had some scheme going in his mind, sharpening his features, and it roused Sebastian's own instincts for trouble. 'You talked rather quietly with Miss Mary Manning today, Barrett.'

Sebastian saw again Mary Manning in his mind, her sweet smile, the gentle touch of her hand on his arm. 'So I did. She was rather unusually intelligent. What of it?'

'A lady like her would probably be something of a challenge.'

'What do you mean?' Nicholas said. He was beginning to look rather alarmed, which Sebastian was sure must be an interesting sign.

'Miss Manning is no flirt, despite her friendship with Lady Louisa,' Gilesworth said. 'She has not been long back in London, due to her father's work, but no one ever has a word of criticism for her. She is pretty, polite, calm, a fine hostess for her father. She couldn't put a dainty slipper wrong.'

Sebastian saw where Gilesworth was going and it made him scowl. He drank down the last of his wine, letting the hazy distance of the alcohol add to his own cold numbness.

'So, in other words, she is exactly what she should be?'

Lord James gave a snort. 'Are any of us what we should be?'

'Exactly,' Gilesworth said. 'Surely no one is perfect inside—even a quiet lady like Miss Manning. She must have a few wild thoughts running through that pretty head.'

Sebastian stared down into the ruby dregs of his glass, but he didn't see the wine. He saw Mary Manning's face, the way she smiled at him, so shy and trusting.

Wild thoughts in her head? Oh, how he would like to know what *those* were! Sebastian almost laughed to imagine Mary Manning going wild, her skirts frothing around her slender legs, her laughter ringing out like music.

And then suddenly he wasn't laughing any longer. The thought of her breaking free, taking him by the hand and drawing him with her into the sunshine, made him feel sad—and also, strangely, hopeful.

'All the ladies seem to talk of nothing but your heroics of late, Barrett,' Gilesworth said. 'Even Miss Manning seemed most fascinated by you today. If anyone could break through such cool perfection, surely it would be you.'

Sebastian shook his head. 'My brother is the one who is interested in Miss Manning.'

Gilesworth and Lord James laughed, as Nicholas watched them, wide-eyed. 'Your brother Lord Henry is surely *not* interested in anything besides his own career. He is as cool-headed as Miss Manning herself. No, I would wager if anyone could break through to the perfect Miss Manning, it would be you.'

'A wager?' Lord James cried. 'Oh, marvellous. I haven't heard an interesting wager in ages.'

Sebastian studied Gilesworth carefully. He didn't quite trust his friend's smile, but he found himself intrigued rather against his will. 'I may be wickedly bored, but I do not wager on a lady's reputation.'

Gilesworth waved his hand in a dismissive gesture. 'No one is suggesting we ruin a lady's fair name! Only that we provide her—and ourselves—with a bit of fun. It has been a most dull Season. Surely even Miss Manning deserves a laugh before she retreats into a blameless life as Lady Henry? If she does become Lady Henry in the end, which I doubt.'

'Then what *are* you suggesting?' Sebastian said in a hard voice.

Gilesworth leaned over the table. 'Just this—fifty guineas says you won't be able to steal a kiss from Miss Manning at the Duchess of Thwaite's ball.'

'Fifty guineas?' Nicholas gasped.

Sebastian did not look away from Gilesworth. 'I told you. I won't ruin a lady's reputation.' Not even to break that terrible coldness around him.

Not even if he was tempted by the thought of kissing Miss Manning. And he *was* tempted. Far more than he cared to admit. Surely the touch of her lips, so sweet and innocent, could make him feel alive again?

'No one would know but us, Barrett,' Gilesworth said. 'And Miss Manning, of course. Give her a thrilling memory. If indeed there is something of fire under her pretty ice, which I am not at all sure of.'

Sebastian sat back in his chair, turning his empty glass around in his hand. There was such a stew of feelings seething inside of him: boredom, desire, intrigue. It was the first spark of warm life he had felt in too long. And yet surely it could not be right.

Maybe he was the rake London society had proclaimed him to be after all.

'Very well,' he said. 'I shall endeavour to kiss the lady just once at the duchess's ball.'

Yet even as he shook hands with Gilesworth to make their devil's bargain, he knew something momentous was going to happen.

Whether for good or ill, he could not say. He only knew Mary Manning had suddenly made him feel alive again.

Chapter Three

Mary watched her reflection in the mirror as her maid put the last touches on her *coiffure* for the Duchess of Thwaite's ball. Usually, she saw none of the elaborate process of braiding and pinning. There were too many other things to go over in her mind. The people her father wanted her to talk to at the party; remembering everyone's names; organising their own dinner parties and who would require return calls and invitations later.

She knew the maids knew their jobs and trusted them to make her look presentable. She knew that she herself could always be called 'presentable'. Pretty enough, always suitably dressed, knowledgeable enough of fashion. She had always been taught to be appropriate.

But she was certainly no stylish beauty like Lady Louisa, or like her own mother. Maria Manning, with her dark Portuguese eyes and musical laugh, had always dazzled everyone. Mary knew she didn't have it in her power to be like that, so she did all she could otherwise. Studied, watched her manners, tried to be helpful.

But tonight she found herself peering into the looking glass as the maid twined a wreath of pink-and-white rosebuds through the braids of her glossy brown hair. She felt so unaccountably nervous tonight, almost unable to sit still. Her thoughts wouldn't stay put on her duties for the duchess's ball, but kept darting all around like shimmering summer butterflies. And she knew exactly why she felt so flighty tonight.

Lord Sebastian Barrett.

Just thinking his name made her want to laugh aloud. Mary found she couldn't quite quell her confusion, that feeling of warm, bubbling anticipation mixed with the twinge of fear. Would he be there that night? She knew Lady Alnworth had said he would. The duchess's ball was *the* event of the Season, and Lord Sebastian was the hero of London at the moment. Surely she would see him there.

Yet if he *were* there, what would she do? What if he talked to her—or didn't talk to her? He was so very handsome, so very sought after, he could certainly have his pick of feminine company.

She remembered the way he had smiled at her in Lady Alnworth's drawing room, the easy way they had talked together. When she was actually with him, there hadn't been this fear. It was only now, thinking about him in the silence of her own room, that she felt so uncertain about everything. And Mary hated being unsure of what to feel, what to do.

She closed her eyes and remembered that morning, when she had gone to take the air with Lady Louisa in the Smythe carriage at the park and she had glimpsed Lord Sebastian in the distance. He had looked so distracted and solemn on his horse, dressed in dark riding clothes, and she had wanted to go to him.

Yet he had seemed somehow to want to remain unobtrusive. He did not wear his dashing regimentals and was alone at the park at a quiet hour. He seemed so distant, as if his thoughts were not on the present moment at all. She hadn't even had the heart to point him out to Louisa.

She had been thrilled at the unexpected sight of him and had longed to call out to him, yet something about his very stillness, his solitary state, had held her back. But then he looked up and saw her, and a smile touched his face. There was only time for him to nod and tip his hat to her, and for her to raise her hand in answer. Then he was lost to sight.

It was that look on his face at that moment that haunted Mary now. That expression of stark—loneliness. It was a feeling she knew very well.

'What do you think, Miss Manning?' the maid said, pulling Mary from her daydreams.

She opened her eyes to look again into the looking glass. She was quite startled by what she saw.

The maid had tried something new with her hair, a twist of braids and curls with the roses and a few pearl pins, and it seemed quite transformative. Her cheeks seemed pinker, her eyes shining.

'You are quite a marvel,' she told the maid, twisting her head to get another view. 'I don't look like myself at all.'

The girl laughed. 'Of course you do, Miss Manning! You just look extra-happy today, if I can be so bold to say so. It must be a very grand ball you're going to tonight.'

'It is indeed grand,' Mary said, but she knew very well it wasn't the prospect of the ball that made her cheeks so pink. She had been to magnificent courtly festivities in St Petersburg, all gilt and pageantry, and they had never filled her with such a tingling excitement of anticipation. It was Lord Sebastian.

There. She had quite admitted it to herself. She was excited to see Lord Sebastian.

Mary laughed, feeling rather giddy.

'Come on, miss, let's get you into your gown now,' the maid said.

Mary nodded, and pushed herself back from her dressing table. Her gaze caught on the miniature portrait of her mother she kept there on a gold stand. Maria Manning had been a true beauty, with a pale oval face and laughing dark eyes, her black hair twined atop her head beneath the intricate lace of her mantilla. Maria's smile seemed to urge her daughter to go dance at the ball, to be bold for the first time in her life. To follow in her mother's passionate Iberian footsteps.

Mary remembered the story of her parents' meeting, of how her father had seen her mother at a ball and they had fallen instantly in love. Mary had always loved hearing those tales and deep down in her most secret heart she had wondered how such a love must feel. As she grew up and saw more of the world, she had known how rare feelings like that really were. She had known she would never find such a thing for herself and would have to be content with a match made of friendship. With a useful, contented marriage.

Now—now it felt almost as if the sun had burst out from behind grey clouds, all surprising and brilliant and glorious. A man like Sebastian Barrett was in the world!

Surely even if he never spoke to her again, that would be enough to give her hope.

But she did hope he would talk to her.

Mary smiled back at her mother and hurried over to let the maid help her into her gown. It was a new creation, straight from the most sought-after modiste in London. Lady Louisa had been quite envious when she heard Mary was to have her new gown in time for the Thwaite ball, but for Mary it had been only one more correct thing to do. She had to look right as her father's hostess.

But now she was very glad she had the new dress. It was much lighter than the heavily embroidered court gowns she had had to wear in St Petersburg, a fluttering, pale-pink silk trimmed with white lace frills and tiny satin rosebuds. The short, puffed sleeves barely skimmed the edges of her shoulders and white satin ribbons fluttered at the high waist. There was even a matching pair of pink-silk slippers, trimmed at the toes with more roses.

Mary couldn't resist a little spin to make the skirts froth up, making the maid laugh. She felt as light and pink and rosy as the gown itself.

She just hoped Lord Sebastian would like it.

* * *

'Mary! Mary, over here!' Lady Louisa called out. Mary glimpsed her friend waving over the heads of the throng crowding into the hall of the Duchess of Thwaite's house, waiting to make their way up the stairs to the ballroom.

Mary waved back, but she couldn't yet push her way through the people pressed around her. Her father held her arm as they had alighted from the carriage, but he was soon called away by some of his diplomatic colleagues. Louisa reached Mary first and drew her behind her to the stairs.

'It's all so exciting, Mary,' Lady Louisa cried, fluffing up her pale-yellow skirts and her bouncing blonde curls. 'I saw Lord Andrewson and his sister go into the ballroom. He sent me flowers earlier, so surely he will ask me to dance! He is so very handsome. Who do *you* want to dance with the very most?'

Mary felt her cheeks turn warm and she looked away. 'Oh—I hardly know.'

But she needn't have feared she would give away her own wild hopes, for Louisa was quickly on to something else, commenting on the gowns of the ladies in the hall below them. Mary only had to smile and nod in reply, which gave her time to peer over the gilded railings to the people just crowding in through the front doors, studying the faces of the newcomers.

Everyone in London society hoped for an invitation to the Thwaite ball and everyone seemed to have appeared for it. The newest, loveliest gowns and finest jewels shimmered in the candlelight. But there was no brilliant flash of a red coat among them. Mary turned away, her smile sinking with a touch of disappointment.

At last they could push their way through the open doors into the duchess's famous ballroom, one of the largest in London. The duchess was also known for having the finest florists and musicians. The long, rectangular room, all gold and white, with a domed ceiling painted with a scene of frolicking gods and cupids against an azure sky, was beautifully decorated with loops of ivy entwined with white roses and gold ribbons. More ivy wreaths hung on the gold silk-covered walls.

Tall glass doors that led on to an open terrace were invitingly ajar.

From a gallery high above, covered with more greenery and roses, an orchestra tuned up for the dancing. Couples made their way on to the patterned parquet floor, laughing and flirting. The sound of happy chatter rose and tangled all around them, so it was impossible to make out a coherent word.

Mary went up on her toes, trying to study the crowd, but just as on the stairs the press and movement were too much to make out anything more than a vivid, shifting kaleidoscope of whites, pinks, blues and yellows, mixed with the dark tones of the men's tailored coats.

She caught a glimpse of her father, standing across the room with the prime minister and a clutch of other politicians. Their faces looked most solemn in the middle of all the merriment. Mary knew he wouldn't need her for some time.

Lady Louisa was quickly claimed for the first dance by her coveted Lord Andrewson. Mary made her way to one of the small gilt-and-satin chairs lined up along the walls, finding a place to sit amid the gossiping chaperons. From there, she had a view of the ballroom doors, where all the new arrivals had to stop.

She was quickly beginning to feel rather foolish, though, waiting for a man who might not even appear.

The musicians launched into the first dance. Mary opened and closed her lace fan, trying to concentrate on the dancers, the beautiful swirl of the ladies' pastel gowns and flashing jewels, the men's fine coats. She tried to distract herself and think of things besides Sebastian Barrett, as she should do at a ball. But nothing quite seemed to work. She felt most unaccountably—fidgety.

She glanced at a tall, ornate clock against the far wall and realised it really was quite early. Many partygoers wouldn't have even finished their dinners yet. She saw Louisa whirl past and gave her a little wave.

Just beyond the dance floor, Mary caught a glimpse of Sebastian Barrett's friends, the ones he had been with at Lady Alnworth's: Lord Paul Gilesworth, Lord James Sackville and Mr Nicholas Warren. Much to her surprise, they were watching *her* in return. Gilesworth even had a quizzing glass to his eye.

Somehow, that regard made her shiver. She felt quite exposed, as if she was wandering in a cold wood alone late at night. She waved her fan harder and looked away, only peeking back once quickly.

Gilesworth was laughing, while Mr Warren shook his head, frowning. Mary realised she rather liked Mr Warren, he seemed sweet, like a puppy dog. But she did not like Lord Paul Gilesworth, his smile never reached his eyes. She couldn't imagine why either of them would watch her.

When she looked their way again, they had vanished into the crowd and there were only the laughing dancers. She felt quite relieved.

The dance ended, and Lord Andrewson left Louisa in the empty chair next to Mary's, promising to fetch them punch and return directly.

'What a crush it is tonight!' Louisa cried, snapping open her own painted-silk fan. 'I can scarcely breathe. I vow my slippers will be in shreds by the end of the evening.'

Mary smiled at her. 'But surely Lord Andrewson is quite the fine dancer.'

Louisa laughed. 'He rather is! But you must dance, too, Mary, the music is too merry not to.' She turned her head to study the room. 'What of Mr Domnhall? Oh, no, he is such a bore—he would put you to sleep even in the middle of a reel, talking of the fishing at his estate in Scotland. Or Lord Sackville? He is rather handsome...'

'Lord Sebastian Barrett,' the duchess's butler suddenly announced. The ballroom doors opened again, and Sebastian Barrett appeared at last. Mary's hand tightened on the carved-ivory sticks of her fan.

He wore his regimentals again, brilliant red-and-gold braid. His hair, that golden-shot-brown that seemed so intriguingly changeable, gleamed like new guineas in the light of the hundreds of candles. It seemed as if time slowed and sped up all at once, the music and laughter becoming a muted blur as Mary watched him. All the light in that dazzling room seemed to gather directly on him, leaving all else in shadow.

He had a mysterious little half-smile as he studied the room before him. His bright, sea-green gaze slid over the assembly—and landed right on Mary. She was so startled she had no time to look away, or even disguise what she was feeling. That sudden rush of pure, molten excitement at seeing him again after all her hopes and fears, the warm giddiness that took hold of her—she feared it was all written on her face.

And after all those years of carefully learning to control her feelings. To always be perfectly, politely smiling. It was most absurd.

The duchess hurried over to greet him, the diamond-sparkled plumes of her elaborate headdress waving, and he was quickly surrounded by the crowd. Mary looked down at the floor and snapped open her fan again.

'Or perhaps you were wise not to dance yet, Mary dear,' Louisa said. 'Not when there are suddenly far more—interesting partners now available.'

Mary glanced up at her friend in surprise. Were her thoughts now so apparent to *every-one*? 'Louisa, I hardly think someone like Lord

Sebastian Barrett would have any shortage of dance partners.'

'La, who said anything about Lord Sebastian?' Louisa cried. 'Yet you had such a look on your face when he came in and I would vow he looked right at *you*. He could do no better for a dinner partner and you, my friend, are much prettier than you ever give yourself credit for. Now, come with me.'

Mary had not an instant to protest as Louisa took her arm and bustled her away from the dowagers' chairs. She pulled Mary through the heavy press of the crowd, so quickly there was no time to look at the people they pushed past. They nearly stumbled over one lady's train and Mary stammered an apology.

'Ah, Lord Sebastian! Surely you remember us. We met at Lady Alnworth's,' Louisa cried. Mary whipped her head back around to find they had landed right in front of Lord Sebastian. The duchess watched them with an astonished look on her face, her gloved hand on the red sleeve of her prized guest, the heroic Lord Sebastian. But Mary barely noticed the social nuances she was usually so carefully attuned to. She could only see him.

'Lady Louisa, Miss Manning,' he said with a bow. 'How very good to see you again. I was hoping you would be here tonight.'

'Were you?' Mary blurted out, then bit her lip.

He smiled down at her, his eyes shimmering. 'Indeed. I enjoyed our talk at Lady Alnworth's. I did glimpse you both at the park, but did not want to interrupt your conversation. Such fine weather this morning.'

Weather? It seemed such a mundane thing to speak of after all Mary's daydreams of his handsome face, his voice, his smile. Yet she was glad of the familiar chatter. It gave her time to compose herself. She surreptitiously smoothed her skirt and gave him a careful smile.

After a few more pleasantries about the warm days and the loveliness of the party, the duchess was reluctantly distracted by even more new arrivals and Louisa tugged on Mary's hand.

'Lord Sebastian, I fear dear Miss Manning was just saying the ballroom is so very crowded she feels rather faint,' Louisa said. 'We were just on our way to seek some fresh air, but I fear I must repair my torn hem.'

Mary looked frantically at Louisa, trying to shake her head in protest. Whatever was her friend trying to do? Her face felt flaming warm all over again. But Louisa just smiled.

'If Miss Manning feels faint, I would be happy to escort her to the terrace for a moment. I am not so fond of crowds myself,' Lord Sebastian said, his smile crinkling the corners of his eyes. It made him look even more handsome.

'Lord Sebastian, really, you must not—' Mary began, breaking off on a gasp as Louisa's grip tightened.

'So very kind, Lord Sebastian!' Louisa said merrily. 'I will join you both in just a moment.'

Louisa spun away and Lord Sebastian held out his red-clad arm to Mary.

She accepted, feeling caught up once again in a hazy, sparkling dream, and let him escort her to the half-open doors of the terrace. She was afraid to look at the people around them, afraid to look up at all, almost fearing it would all vanish.

She was also afraid he had been caught by Louisa's machinations, that he had a thousand places where he would rather be. Yet he gave no sign of resentment at all, no indication he wanted to leave her in the nearest corner at the first chance. He held tight to her arm, smiling solicitously as if he did indeed think she might faint. He talked in a low, deep voice of more light things such as the weather and the music, things she only had to make blessedly short answers to.

She glanced at him secretly from the corner of her eye, examining his sharply chiselled profile. There was no sign of what she thought she had glimpsed at Lady Alnsworth's, that stark second of loneliness, and then in that brief glimpse at the park. That raw, burning solitariness she herself hid so deep inside.

They slipped through the doors on to the terrace. It was an unusual space in a London house, a wide marble walkway with carved stone balustrades looking down on to a manicured garden. Down there, Chinese lanterns strung along the trees gleamed on flower beds and pale classical statues.

Along the terrace itself, potted plants created intimate little pathways, with chairs tucked behind their leafy shelter, perfect for quiet conversations. A few other couples strolled there, pale glimpses between the dark green.

The hush after the roar of the ballroom was almost deafening.

'If I had my own house, I would make a space much like this,' Lord Sebastian said, his voice quiet, with a rather musing tone, as if he was somewhere far away.

Mary glanced up at him, startled to see how serious he looked as he studied the garden. 'Your own house, Lord Sebastian?'

He looked down at her, a half-smile on his lips. 'I could hardly add it to my father's house. He would consider a terrace a great frivolity.'

'I sometimes think about what I would like to have in my own home, as well. I have never really had one, we move about so much. No one asks what colours one might like in lodgings! But some day…'

'Some day a real home of one's own would be nice.'

'Yes, indeed.'

They stopped at the end of the terrace, where two marble balustrades met and a set of stone steps led down to the garden. The corner was sheltered by a thick bank of potted palms. It was quiet there, no sound but the faint echo of music and laughter from the ballroom, the whisper of a breeze through the trees.

Mary could almost imagine they were alone there. It was disconcerting, making her shiver with nervousness—yet it was also rather alluringly lovely. In the crowded ballroom, she had felt so alone, as she often did at large parties. Here, with just him, she didn't feel alone at all.

'A terrace like this could be so lovely for a luncheon party on a warm day. Or maybe a small dance party in the moonlight for just a few friends,' she said, watching the way the breeze danced on the flowers.

'A home where one's true friends could gather would be a wondrous thing indeed. I have lived in camp tents so much of late, that—' He broke off with a rueful laugh. 'Forgive me, Miss Manning, I must be so boring. I get carried away with my own thoughts far too often these days.'

'I'm not bored at all,' Mary said. Rather, she was most fascinated by this tiny glimpse of the man behind the heroic Lord Sebastian Barrett. A man who might long for a real home just as she did.

'Once, while we were camped at a field in the middle of nowhere, I saw a constellation of stars I had never noticed before,' he said. 'Like a diamond necklace, all sparkling against the darkness. It was wondrous.'

He looked up into the sky and Mary did the same. The darkness was just as it always was in London—hazy, with only a few very bold stars managing to peek through. Yet she could imagine what he had once seen in that field. A dazzling sparkle of lights blazing their way across a black-velvet sky, before the unimaginable carnage of a battlefield.

'Do you ever dream of what it might be like to float up there among the stars, all untethered from—everything,' she said fancifully.

She was surprised at herself, at her sudden dreams. 'To just—be.'

He looked down at her. He looked surprised, too, his smile so very real this time. He slowly nodded. 'Of course. Especially here in London.'

'Here?' she asked. 'Not on campaign?'

His smile turned lopsided, his eyes distant. 'It sounds strange, I know. But with my regiment, I knew what was expected of me, what I was meant to do and how to do it well. I knew what was thought of me, what I thought of the world around me. Here—here I seem to know so little. It's London that has become the alien world.'

Mary nodded. It was how she had felt for so long, ever since they came back to London, that she no longer knew where her place was. 'I have never been in battle, thankfully, but it's been a long time since I lived in London. My father and I have been our own small world for so long, the one thing I take from place to place, and it's hard to know quite what to do now. I know I *am* English, that this is meant to be my home, yet—'

She broke off, unsure of what she was saying. These were thoughts she had kept pressed down so hard, not even daring to think them to herself. Her father had enough to worry about—what with losing her beloved mother and the vital importance of his work, he couldn't worry about her, too.

Yet the strangeness of being back in England, the lonely moments—how could anyone understand?

But it seemed that, of all people, the handsome Sebastian Barrett *did* understand. His smile widened, a gorgeous white flash in the shadows, and he nodded. 'It's as if everyone here was speaking a foreign language, one I can only decipher on the surface and speak well enough to play my part passably.'

Mary was fascinated. He was the hero of society! How could he be lost? Yet she could see the dark gleam in his eye. 'What part is that, Lord Sebastian?'

He leaned his forearms on the marble balustrade and stared out at the dark garden. 'Oh, we all have our parts here, don't you agree, Miss Manning? Most people have played them so long they can't even look past them any longer. They have *become* what they are meant to be. When I was with my regiment, I felt that sense of rightness, that sense that I knew my duty and could carry it out well. It was a feeling everyone should have at some time in their lives, even though it might mean others then carry far too many expectations. But some of us *do* wonder what it would be like to float among the stars and just be, as you say.'

'Free to find our real selves?' Mary thought that a most astonishing, and delightful, idea. She longed to know more of his life in the Army, more of what that feeling of 'rightness' could entail.

'What would you do, then, Miss Manning?'

She studied him in the half-light, the sculpted angles of his handsome face, then glanced back up at the sky. 'I hardly know. I have worked for my family for so long.'

'So you would be a diplomat, like your father?'

Mary laughed. 'There are certainly things I do like about my father's work. Doing good for one's country, seeking peace, seeing fas-

cinating places, meeting different people—
I do like those. But there is one thing I wish
was different.'

'And what is that?'

Mary smiled up at him. Could he be truly
interested in her own musings, her own inner
thoughts? He looked back down at her, his
smile vanished. 'A real home. We have moved
about so much, I can't even remember what a
place that was truly my own would be like.'

'A cottage in the woods?'

'Perhaps,' she answered with a laugh. 'A
half-timbered cottage, with a little rose garden,
perhaps a cat on the front steps. Or maybe a
shining white castle on a mountaintop. A place
for a large family.'

'A family,' he murmured and Mary was sure
she saw a strange shadow cross his face.

'What would you want, Lord Sebastian?'

He laughed, that shadow gone before she
was even sure she saw it. 'A castle on a mountain sounds rather ideal. A place far from my
family.'

Mary was suddenly reminded he was Lord
Henry Barrett's brother, and she shivered guilt-

ily. 'Are you not happy to be back with your family now?'

'As happy as most people are with their families, I would imagine, Miss Manning. I am very glad of the friends and parties I have found in London, the distractions.'

Mary stared out into the garden. 'Diversion, yes. You don't have to stay out here with me, Lord Sebastian. I know many people will want to talk to you tonight.'

He gave her another smile, one so sweet, so alluring, it made her fall back against the chilly stone balustrade, unsure her legs would hold her upright now.

'But I like it better here, talking to one person,' he said. 'You are most unexpected, Miss Manning.'

'Me? Unexpected?' she said, surprised. He was certainly the one who was unexpected— and even more intriguing than he had been before. There seemed to be so much hidden behind his dashing façade. 'On the contrary, Lord Sebastian. I am most ordinary.'

'Ordinary is certainly the very last thing you are.' He reached for her hand, holding it gently between his fingers, as if it was a delicate, precious piece of glass. 'Is it so unbelievable that I would rather be out here talking to you, watching the stars with you, than be packed into a crowded ballroom?'

Mary couldn't stop staring at his hand on hers. His was so strong, sun-browned and scarred, against her white glove. 'Yes,' she blurted.

He laughed and raised her hand to his lips for a quick kiss. His mouth was warm and surprisingly soft through her thin glove, making her shiver. He looked so golden in the moonlight, so like a dream.

'How little you do know me, Miss Manning,' he said. Something like a flash of sadness, regret, passed over his face.

'I don't know you at all, surely, Lord Sebastian.' And now she wanted to—all too much.

'I feel as if I no longer know myself at all. I have done some wretched things, I fear,' he said, pressing her palm to his cheek.

'Wretched?' Mary whispered. 'Whatever do you mean?'

He shook his head. 'I wish I could tell you—

and I hope you never know. Yet I think you should see something…'

His expression looked so very far away, Mary was overwhelmed with the feeling of a bittersweet melancholy. She only knew she wanted to make him feel better, soothe whatever pain it was that seemed to burrow inside of him, beyond that golden beauty.

She didn't know what else to do, so she went up on tiptoe and kissed him. She knew little of kissing outside of books, so her touch was soft, tentative, full of the hope she could distract him. But his lips parted under hers as his breath caught in surprise and the taste of him filled her with a warm rush of delight.

His hands closed over her shoulders and at first she feared he might push her away. Then he groaned, a hungry, wild sound deep in his throat, and his arms came around her in a hard embrace. He dragged her closer to his hard, warm chest and she went most willingly.

His mouth hardened on hers, his tongue tracing the soft curve of her lips before plunging inside to taste her deeply, hungrily. She wanted so much, more of him. She had never felt like that before, as if she soared up into the stars in truth.

She felt him press her back against the balustrade, his open mouth sliding from hers to trace her jaw, her arched neck. He touched the sensitive little spot behind her ear lightly with the tip of his tongue, making her laugh.

How wondrous kissing was! Why had she not known that before? Or was it only *him* that made it so wonderful? She reached up to twine her fingers in his hair and pulled him up to kiss her lips again. He went most eagerly, his kisses catching fire with a need that made her own burn even hotter.

'Mary,' he whispered against her skin and the one word was so full of deep hidden meaning.

She pressed herself even closer to him, wanting to be nearer and nearer. Wanting so much of—she knew not what. She had fallen into the stars.

'Oh, bravo, Sebastian! That was quick work indeed.'

The sudden sound of a gleeful voice felt like a shower of cold water raining down on the golden sunshine of that kiss. Mary stumbled back from Sebastian and would have fallen over the balustrade if he hadn't still held on to her arm. She physically ached, as if she had taken a sudden and sharp tumble.

She peered past his shoulder to find three men watching them—Lord Paul Gilesworth, Nicholas Warren and Lord James Sackville, who had been with Sebastian at Lady Alnworth's house. It was Giles who had spoken and he watched them with a most repulsive, artificial smile. Mr Warren, to his dubious credit, looked red-faced and appalled, while Lord James laughed.

Mary shook her head. This was surely a nightmare. It simply had to be. Only a moment before, she had felt more burningly alive than ever before. Now she felt cold, distant from the whole scene before her, as if she watched it in a play.

What had seemed such a sparkling, wondrous fairy tale had become something strange and ugly. She closed her eyes and prayed for delivery from that bad dream. She felt his hand on her arm and even it was not like before. Now it felt like a shackle.

When she opened her eyes, it was all still there. The men looking at her, Gilesworth looking horribly triumphant. She was trapped, frozen. After so many years of being proper, being careful, she had made one small misstep and been caught. It was a horrible feeling.

She waited for Sebastian to say something, for the appalling embarrassment to vanish, but that one terrible instant seemed to stretch on and on.

Then Gilesworth's words, *all* his words, crashed into her mind.

Quick work indeed.

Could that mean—was it really possible? Had Sebastian *meant* to seduce her into kissing him, for the amusement of his friends?

She swung around to look at him, horrified. He stared back at her, his face wary, unreadable. The man who had talked to her of the stars, who had listened to her confidences and kissed her so sweetly, had vanished.

'Is…is it…' she stammered. She wasn't even sure what she was trying to say. Every word she ever knew had fled from her mind. She felt her cheeks flame with red-hot shame, yet at the same time she was frozen. She could only stare up at Sebastian. She couldn't see his eyes in the shadows.

'You should be quite proud, Miss Manning, to have gained the attention of such a hero as our Lord Sebastian,' Gilesworth said smugly. 'We weren't sure the two of you really had it in you to be so bold. But I see that for fifty guineas...'

Fifty guineas? Were they *paying* Sebastian to kiss her?

Fool, fool, her mind screamed at her. She had never felt so silly, so stupid before in her life.

'Mary, no, please...' Sebastian began, his voice rough and hoarse.

But Mary couldn't bear to hear him say anything, for him to make excuses or, far worse, laugh at her. She felt like the sky, so beautiful with those shimmering stars, was crashing atop her.

She shook her head and pulled her arm free of his touch. What had felt so warm, so safe, now felt like ice. She couldn't bear to be near him a moment longer, to face the laughter of his friends. She spun around and ran towards the doors into the ballroom, hardly knowing where she was going. She heard Gilesworth's laughter chasing her.

Only when she saw the bright lights, the blur of the spinning dancers, did she realise she was in no fit state to face a crowd. Even if word of that kiss, that horrid bet, spread, she would have to hold her head up in a dignified play-act. She veered around to the side of the house and found a footman to direct her to the ladies' retiring room.

It was thankfully quiet in the small sitting room. Mary ducked behind a screen to take a deep breath, to close her eyes and try to slow down her racing thoughts. As she smoothed her hair and straightened her skirt, she heard the door open and other ladies' gowns rustling into the room amid a cloud of laughter. She had to compose herself, then find her father and go home immediately.

The most handsome rogue in London. Mary bit her lip to keep from laughing aloud

in a rather bitter fashion. They were utterly
right, on both counts. Sebastian Barrett was
devilishly handsome—and a terrible rogue,
with no concern for ladies' feelings. Mary
was sure she should have realised that, should
have realised that his attentions were all a
terrible jest. Men like him had no interest in
women like her.

She would never forget that again.

'Mary!' Sebastian called, but she was already gone, vanished into the darkness of the
evening like a fluttering pink butterfly. His
own head felt cursedly clouded, hazy with the
unexpected delight of that kiss, and he wasn't
fast enough to catch her. He had started to tell
her the truth, had *wanted* to tell her, and yet it
all came much too late.

Gilesworth caught Sebastian's arm as he
started after her, and tossed a heavy purse of
clanking coins at his chest. Sebastian let them
fall to the terrace stones as he stared into Gilesworth's smirking face.

How had he ever befriended such a man,
even in his desperation to forget battle? He

had let boredom draw him into a vile scheme and now he bitterly rued the day.

All he could see was Mary's face, pale and shocked in the moonlight as she ran away from him. For one perfect moment, as he held her slender, trembling body in his arms, he had forgotten the men he had lost in battle, forgotten his family and London society, and the terrible, numb aimlessness of life. *She* made him forget, made things seem new and bright again.

It was something he hadn't expected at all, something startling. That awakening to sensation again, with the soft touch of her lips, the faint scent of her sweet rose perfume. And it had been shattered all too quickly, snatched away, and he had little but himself to blame. He had taken Gilesworth's ridiculous wager, and now he had wounded the sweetest lady he had ever met.

He reached out and grabbed Gilesworth by the front of his immaculate evening coat, erasing the man's hideous smirk.

'You will never speak of this to anyone,' Sebastian said, in a low, steady voice. He wouldn't let his burning anger overwhelm him now; he had to help Mary however he could and stemming any gossip was only the first step. 'If I even hear that you have so much as uttered Miss Manning's name, I shall make you sorry you were ever born.'

Gilesworth's self-satisfied smirk vanished, replaced by fear barely masked by a scowl. 'Now, listen here, Barrett. It was all just a bit of fun, and you—'

'It is in no way a "bit of fun", and I was a bloody, foxed fool to ever involve myself in such a vile scheme,' Sebastian said. Inside, the dark flood of self-disgust threatened to drown him, but outwardly he stayed cold and calm. It was the hard lesson of battle. 'But it is over now. You will leave Miss Manning in peace. Is that understood?'

He swept a cold glance over all of them. Lord James swallowed hard and nodded, and Nicholas Warren looked red-faced and ap-palled. Gilesworth scowled, as if he would argue and force Sebastian to challenge him to a duel or something equally ridiculous, but when Sebastian's fist tightened in the twist of his coat, he sullenly agreed.

Sebastian pushed the man away and hurried to the house to find Mary. She was nowhere to be seen in the ballroom, and her friend Lady Louisa said she thought Mary had already summoned her carriage to return home.

Her smile turned teasing as she looked up at him. 'But I am sure if she knew you were looking for her, she would never have left so quickly.'

Sebastian knew he had to neutralise any gossip now, even with Mary's friends. He smiled back at her, a careless, casual smile. 'I had hoped for a dance with Miss Manning, but I see I was too slow. At the next ball, then.'

He bowed and left her, even though she looked as if she wanted to say something more to him. He found a footman near the duchess's staircase and the servant verified Lady Louisa's words, that Miss Manning had called for her carriage and departed in rather a hurry. Sebastian rushed to the street outside, but there was no glimpse of the departing Manning carriage, even in the distance.

He would have to go to her home in the

morning, at a proper hour, and make his apologies. He could only hope she would forgive him.

Chapter Four

'Oh, Miss Manning! Thank heavens you're here,' Mary's maid cried, leaping out of her seat in the hall of the Manning house as Mary stepped inside. The floor was piled with crates and trunks. 'Your father has been asking for you most urgently.'

'My father?' Surprise and worry jolted Mary out of the dismal reflections that had been running through her head ever since she had left the duchess's ball. She had thought it was rather odd that her father would leave the ball early and send the carriage back for her, but she had been too busy chastising herself for ever trusting Sebastian Barrett.

She quickly handed her shawl to the maid

and followed the butler down the corridor to her father's library.

She found her father standing in the midst of more crates, sorting his books and papers as more of the servants hurried around him taking paintings from the walls and draping the furniture in canvas covers. Candles were lit everywhere, casting a flicker over all the frantic activity. She noticed how tired her father looked and now concern replaced the hurt and embarrassment.

Mary was bewildered. It was nearly the middle of the night—what could be happening?

'Papa? What is going on?' Mary asked, making her way between the uneven stacks of crates. She caught sight of herself in the looking glass on the wall, just before a footman threw a cloth over it. Her hair was tousled, her cheeks overly pink.

Luckily, her father did not seem to notice. He shoved a stack of books into her hands and vaguely gestured at one of the boxes.

'I am very glad you're here, Mary,' he said. 'There is not an instant to lose! We must leave in the morning. I've instructed the maids to start packing your gowns.'

'In the morning!' Mary cried, even more confused. Had he found out about what happened at the ball, that she had disgraced herself? 'Papa, whatever do you mean? Where are we going? Surely it is not so bad yet we must flee from gossip…'

'Gossip?' Her father turned to peer at her closer, his arms full of more papers. 'Is there gossip about Portugal? How very odd. The prime minister said haste and secrecy were of utmost importance, but I wouldn't have thought London society would care. Not yet.'

'Portugal?' Mary's head was spinning. 'Perhaps we should slow down for a moment, so you can tell me what exactly is happening. A half-hour ago I was at a ball…' Kissing Sebastian Barrett, but her father didn't need to know *that*. 'Now you say we must pack and be gone by morning.'

Her father gave a wry laugh and leaned down to give her cheek a quick kiss. 'You are quite right, my dear. It is all quite odd, but surely you have become rather accustomed to that in this strange life of ours.'

Mary nodded. Strange things *had* always happened in her life. New nurseries, new nannies, balls, receptions, new customs, new manners. She had been able to weather them all, thanks to her parents' example. But now she had no idea how to manage her own feelings. Her own mistakes.

Her father took her hand and led her to a quiet spot near one of the windows, away from the rush and noise of the footmen carrying away the crates. 'I spoke to the prime minister tonight and he says it is most vital that I be in Portugal as soon as possible. The Portuguese have been trying to maintain neutrality between England and France, but Napoleon's diplomats have been making very threatening noises to Dom Joao. Lord Strangford has been made Britain's representative to the royal court there, but the prime minister wants someone with a great knowledge of the country to join him and advise him.'

'As you do, because of Mama,' Mary said. She thought of the short time they had been in Portugal when she was a child, the sun and light of it, her mother's laughter. Surely it could be a refuge of sorts, somewhere far from England where she would make no more romantic mistakes.

'As I do, yes. It will be a great challenge, I confess, perhaps the greatest I have faced in my career.' Her father sighed, his face a bit weary. He reached out and gently touched Mary's cheek. 'I am sorry, my dear. We have barely settled in London and now I must drag you away again. Perhaps you would rather stay here, maybe with your friend Lady Louisa?'

'Oh, no, Papa,' Mary cried. 'I want to go with you, of course. I should love to see Portugal again and you will need someone to make sure you eat properly.'

He laughed. 'And I confess I would be most lonely without you. But I can't help but wonder—are you quite all right?'

Mary was afraid the events at the ball could somehow show on her face and the last thing her father needed was more worries. 'Of course, Papa. I must be a bit tired after the dancing.'

He looked as if he wanted to say something

else, but the butler called him away with a question about the packing. Mary hurried out of the library and upstairs to her chamber, past several servants carrying out more trunks.

She paused at the window on the landing to peer out at the night. The sky was just beginning to lighten at the edges, a pale grey that would see them gone blessedly soon. Against her will, a vision of Sebastian Barrett flashed through her mind. Those jewel-green eyes, that had seemed so sad just before he kissed her. The rush of hot, burning pain when she realised she was only a joke to him.

She pushed the memory away and rushed on towards her room. It felt horribly like running away, but she was very glad of the sudden departure to Portugal. There, she wouldn't have to worry about seeing Lord Sebastian, facing what her foolish infatuation had led her into.

And, hundreds of miles away, she wouldn't have to face being led into temptation by him all over again...

Sebastian knocked on the Mannings' door again and listened to the hollow echo inside.

He stepped back on the walkway and peered up at the house, his hat in one hand and a bouquet of roses in the other. It looked as if all the windows were shuttered, the doors locked.

His heart sank. Where could they be? Surely it had only been last night he saw Mary at the ball and everything went so disastrously wrong. He *had* gone back to his lodgings and drank rather too much wine after he lost her in the crowd, but surely he had not lost *that* much time?

Even the wine hadn't been able to give him sleep. Just like so many other nights since he came back to England, he sat awake into the dawn hours, yet last night it wasn't the haunting thoughts of battle that kept him up. It was the memory of Miss Manning's eyes, the way she looked up at him just before she kissed him, so full of wonder that she made him feel it, too. Made the night seem new.

And the shadow in those same eyes when she realised the truth. When she realised the damnable cad he had somehow become.

The truth of what he had done, his appallingly ungentlemanly behaviour, had shocked him out of his hazy, pain-filled memories as nothing else could. He hated what he had become, how near he had come to hurting a sweet lady like Mary Manning.

As soon as he had pulled back the curtains to let the light of day wash over his aching head and carry away the cobwebs of the night, he had known what he had to do. He had to go to Miss Manning immediately, apologise and beg for her forgiveness.

Ask her to help him somehow find his way back into the world. After that kiss, the warm newness of it, he was sure she was the only one who could help him. And he had to erase those shadows he had created in her sweet, beautiful eyes.

But how could he make amends if he couldn't find her?

He knocked on the door again, only to be greeted with the same—no answer. Some of his eager certainty turned chilly.

The downstairs servants' door to the house next door opened and a maid appeared on the front steps with a bucket and scrub brush. She gave him a curious glance.

'Looking for the Mannings, are you, sir?' she asked.

He gave her a relieved smile. 'Yes, indeed. Though it seems I must come back later, since the door knocker is off.'

'Won't do you any good, sir, as I think they left this morning.'

'Left? For good?'

'Oh, yes. Carts came and hauled off boxes and trunks before it was even light outside. That happened to the last people who lived there, too, but they ran off from the debt collectors. My master says the Mannings were just sent off to a new posting.' She gave a doubtful frown under the frills of her cap.

Off to a new posting. Already? How could that be? Sebastian felt the heat of an urgent need to find Miss Manning right away, before she left for good.

He knew of one person who always seemed to know what was happening with the Foreign Office—his father. Sebastian quickly thanked the maid and hurried back to his phaeton, set on going to his parents' house in Portman Square immediately. His father would be certain Sebastian had messed something up, again, and indeed he had.

But then he had to find Miss Manning.

'It is good you are here, Sebastian,' his father said, barely looking up from the papers scattered across his desk as Sebastian knocked at his library door.

Sebastian was surprised and brought up short on his urgent errand. His father was seldom happy to see him at the family domicile. Even after he had returned from the battlefield and his father admitted that Sebastian's Army life had been a credit to their family after all, his father had spoken of little but his own work at the Foreign Office. 'Indeed?'

'Yes. Henry has been ill this week and there is much work to be done. Several people have been sent to new, vital postings and I must see that these messages go to them immediately. You can deliver some of them, surely? Find out from Henry if he has messages to send, as well.'

Sebastian was even more startled. 'You want *my* help, Father?'

His father looked up, blinking behind his spectacles, almost as if he just realised Sebastian was there. 'You're here, so of course you'll do. I told you, Henry is ill and your eldest brother is still in the country looking after the estate. You can make yourself useful, for once.'

Sebastian laughed wryly. That was all he *could* do, really, when it came to his family. Laugh—and go his own way. His world had been designated the dust and roar of battle long ago, far from the darker world of his father and Henry, the world of diplomacy.

The world of Miss Manning and her father.

He remembered his true errand at his father's library, to find out what had happened to the Mannings, and he brushed away his irritation. 'So your diplomatic friends are being shuffled off to new ports, are they?'

His father glared at him. 'You have never shown an interest in them before.'

Sebastian shrugged. He had to keep up his careless façade; he could never let his father see that something mattered to him, especially if that something was a respectable young lady.

'These are interesting times, are they not? One never knows when the Army will be called out next. I met your friends the Mannings at the Alnworth ball.'

'Did you indeed? Sir William has been sent to Lisbon. That idiot Prince Joao has been wavering in his alliance and must be brought back most firmly to England's side. The loss of Portuguese New World ports at this time would be disastrous. Sir William is the man for the job.'

'To Portugal?' Sebastian said, his mind racing. Mary Manning would be well on her journey now—too far out of the reach of his apologies. He had to find her somehow.

His father waved him away and turned back to his papers. 'I must finish this. Go see your brother and be on your way, Sebastian.'

Sebastian hardly noticed his father's curt dismissal, so accustomed was he to this behaviour. He thought perhaps Henry would know more of Miss Manning. They were rumoured to maybe make a match of it, after all, and Henry seemed much more the sort of man Sir William would want for his daughter—on the surface, anyway.

He left his father's library and made his way up the stairs to the corridor where Henry had his rooms. On the staircase, he was suddenly caught by the painted eyes of the ancestral portraits hung on the red-painted walls. A long line of them, all the way back to a Barrett who represented Charles I in Venice, who served England so well behind the scenes. Who excelled at saving their country time and again.

When he was a child, he always thought they seemed to sniff at him disapprovingly. They didn't seem to have changed much over the years.

He dashed past them and knocked on Henry's sitting-room door. 'Come in!' Henry ordered, and when he saw it was his brother rather than a servant, he merely added, 'Oh. It is you.'

'Your brother, home from the wars,' Sebastian answered lightly. 'Father is sending off messengers hither and yon, he wanted to see if you had anything to add.'

'Just a moment, then.' Henry turned back to his desk. Like their father, he was tall and slim, with curling hair and spectacles over his faraway blue eyes. But Sebastian noticed suddenly that Henry also seemed pale, a warm wrap closely tucked around his shoulders despite the sunny day. Sebastian wondered with a worried pang if his brother was indeed ill, but he knew Henry would welcome no such queries.

'Father says all your diplomatic friends are scattering across the Continent, gathering in reluctant allies,' Sebastian said.

'I doubt he would put it quite like that,' Henry muttered. 'But, yes. We must all do our duty now.'

'He said Sir William Manning has been sent to Portugal.'

'It is of vital importance now.'

'So it seems. But I heard a rumour you might miss Sir William's daughter when she is gone.'

Henry gave a humourless laugh. 'Miss Mary Manning? I had thought of her, of course. Our fathers have long known each other and she knows what a life such as ours entails. She wouldn't be too tiresome.'

Sebastian felt a flare of anger on the lovely

Miss Mary's behalf—only to push it away, knowing he had no right. *He* was the one she should rightfully be furious with, of course. 'I saw her at the ball last night. She was very pretty.'

'She is all right, but that hardly matters, does it? I must find a suitable bride one day and she is one of the ladies who would be suitable. But right now I cannot think of such things.' Henry glanced up from his letter. 'Nor should you. Duty is paramount right now, Seb.'

'You needn't lecture me about duty, Henry. I have served England with my own blood and will again.'

Henry studied him closely. 'We all do what we can, I suppose. Here, give these letters to Father. And I hope you are not tempted to add a little line to Miss Manning. Ladies like that are not for such as you, Brother. Besides, perhaps she will be better off in Portugal. I hear her own mother was from Lisbon.'

'Oh, believe me, I know that she is not for me very well indeed.' Sebastian took the letter from his brother, looking into Henry's cold blue eyes, and turned on his heel to leave the room. His brother had long been studious, long been focused on following their father's footsteps, but when had be become so very distant? So hardened to people like Miss Manning, seeing only her 'usefulness'?

Then again—Sebastian knew he himself had been no better. Surely his brother was right. Now was not the time to chase Miss Manning and make her listen to his poor excuses. She had her own family to think of now, her own work, and he had his.

Perhaps only through his work could he one day make her see how sorry he was and how he would work to erase that one night. If only he could some day see her again.

'Sebastian!' Sebastian heard Nicholas Warren call from across the street as he stepped out of his father's house. He glanced over to find his friend hurrying between the carriages and horses, his hat threatening to fly away in the breeze, and the sight actually made him start to smile. Nicholas often had that effect on people.

But his brief smile faded as he saw Nicholas's face. His friend was usually quick to smile, yet today he looked solemn as a funeral, and Sebastian was reminded sharply of that disagreeable scene at the ball—as if he could forget it. He would never forget the darkness that came into Mary Manning's bright eyes.

'Were you calling on your father?' Nicholas asked. He glanced up at the Barrett house, looking as if the bricks and stone could suddenly sprout teeth and bite him. Most of Sebastian's friends seemed to have that reaction.

'Yes, duty done for the day. I was on my way back to my lodgings.' Sebastian almost suggested they go to the club for a claret, but then he remembered too clearly what had happened the last time they were there.

Nicholas nodded. 'Surely too early for the club,' he said, as if he had read Sebastian's thoughts. 'Shall I walk with you? I am supposed to escort my sister to the milliner later and I'd rather like to put off that errand for as long as I can. Can I walk with you for a time?'

'Of course,' Sebastian answered. 'If you can bear my company right now.'

Nicholas was quiet for a moment as they made their way along the walkway. 'Do you mean because of what happened at the ball? Surely it was my fault for introducing you to such a bounder as Gilesworth. I know you haven't been, well, quite yourself since you returned to London and I thought the chaps at the club might amuse you. I'm sorry for that.'

'It is not your fault in the least, Nick,' Sebastian said, feeling even worse now that he knew he had hurt and disappointed one of his best friends as well as Miss Manning. 'You are quite right—I have not been myself since I left my regiment. I have been behaving terribly, and after what happened I felt as if I woke from a nightmare to find I had done terrible things in my sleep. You tried to stop that wretched wager from ever happening and I thank you for that.'

Nicholas reached up to fiddle with his hat, his face gong a bit red. 'Well. Yes. What shall you do now?'

'I wanted to apologise to Miss Manning myself, but it seems she has gone away. One day, though, when that chance comes, I hope I can tell her I was not myself and prove it to her.' An image of Mary Manning's face flashed in his mind again, her shy smile, the glow of her eyes.

'A goal more worthy of you, I must say,' Nick said encouragingly. 'How will you do that?'

Sebastian shrugged. 'Return to my regiment, I suppose. Do my duty the best I can.' He paused, trying to collect his thoughts. 'If you ever happen to run into the Mannings in your own work…'

'Shall I pass on a message?'

Sebastian was tempted, but he could imagine the dismay on Miss Manning's face to hear his name. Surely she could only think any secondhand words most insincere. 'No. Just speak kindly of me to Miss Manning. If you can bear to.'

They walked along in silence for a few more moments and Sebastian thought of her. The warmth and welcome of her kindness after his rocky homecoming, the way she made him think of the more pleasant things in life when he was with her. He had ruined all that much too quickly. But if he had learned one thing from his Army life, it was that men could always redeem themselves if they wanted to, if they tried. They could always be better. And he would try to do that, if only in memory of Miss Manning.

Chapter Five

Lisbon, two years later

It sounded as if the world was cracking open.

Another deafening peal of thunder broke over the tiled roof of the Manning house in the Baixa district of Lisbon, making Mary's lady's maid scream and duck down to cover her head.

'Mother of heaven, *senhorita*, but it is the French, come to murder us in our beds!' she cried.

'Don't be silly, Adriana,' Mary said sternly, though she was far from feeling certain herself. She had to force herself to stay with her embroidery by the fire and not leap up at every noise. True, it was just a storm rolling in from the hills—this time. 'It is only rain.'

A gust of wind caught at one of the shutters, making Adriana scream again. Mary jumped up and ran to catch it.

The chilly autumn wind rushing over the rooftops was a relief after being closed inside all day, ever since her father received an urgent message summoning him to the royal palace at Mafra, outside the city. He'd warned Mary to stay in, to keep the servants calm, but that was becoming harder and harder to obey. The whole city felt as if it would burst at any moment from the terrible strain of fear and uncertainty. The storm only made everything worse.

Mary leaned out the window, letting the cold, damp wind catch at her loosely braided hair, the fringe of her shawl. Their house was on a small plaza, like so many in Lisbon, a tall, whitewashed structure along a cobblestone square with a communal fountain at its centre. Over the steep red-tiled roofs she could see the purple outlines of the hills against the night sky, inky and impenetrable. The storm clouds scuttled past overhead, casting shadows over the moon. Only sizzling, silvery bolts of lightning split the gloom.

Mary shivered and pulled her shawl closer around her shoulders. Usually the nights in Lisbon were full of sound. Music from the salons, their windows thrown wide to the flower-scented breezes. Laughter from the people parading together around the plazas. Lights sparkling in long, snaking rivers up the narrow lanes into the hills. It was one of the things she loved about the city, the birthplace of her beautiful mother. She tried to write of it in her long letters to Louisa back in England, to show it all to her friend. The laughter and fire of it, the warmth and life. So different from London, especially the London from Louisa's return letters, a place of assemblies and plays with the same people every night. Compared to that, Lisbon had felt so—freeing.

But now the city was completely transformed, as if a wicked fairy had cast a dark spell over it all. The plaza was deserted, the fountain gone still. Many of the doors and windows were barricaded, some of the houses deserted as families fled to the countryside. Even the church bells were quiet. No one knew what would happen next. It was quite certain Portugal's hard-fought neutrality between England and France could no longer hold. But which way would things tumble?

Mary curled her fingers into the wood of the windowsill, forcing herself to breathe deeply, to remain still. With her father, she had seen the careful diplomatic dance many times before, yet it had never felt so very urgent.

She glanced up at the dark hills and imagined the armies that were on the move just beyond them, on the Iberian plains. Was Sebastian Barrett among them, dashing in his red coat, urging his men onward to defeat the French? Or was he already dead on some distant battlefield, once more lauded as great hero in London? The thought of his spirit being gone from the world made her shiver.

'Stop it, Mary,' she whispered to herself. She had to push away memories of Sebastian, as she always did when he slid unbidden into her mind, her dreams. Usually she was much too busy to let him there again, to let him charm her all over again. But sometimes, especially in tense, quiet moments like this one, he slipped back in. Taunting her with how foolish she had once been.

She had let no one court her since London, since she let herself care for Lord Sebastian Barrett, let herself believe his lies. Lord Henry Barrett had married someone else and had passed away from a fever on a posting to Madeira, news which her father had received sadly. Lord Henry had written to her once or twice, but his words on the page had been as stiff and dutiful as their meetings in London had been. After she had danced with Sebastian, she had known that any marriage based on business, on abrupt convenience, could never be for her, even though such romantic feelings had ended badly. She thought perhaps she would end a spinster, keeping house for her father always. But she had heard little of Sebastian in all those months. Louisa had once given an offhand mention in one of her letters that it was rumoured Sebastian would marry his sister-in-law's sister, some viscount's daughter, but naught had come of it. Mary hadn't wanted to ask too much, to seem too eager. And she half feared to hear bad news. Even though he had hurt her...

The thought of him being gone was still too painful. He had shown her a new way of feeling, even if it had only been for a moment.

Lightning suddenly crashed out of the sky, a sizzling lavender-white flash, and Mary drew back, startled. Thunder rattled the roof tiles and the first cold drops of rain touched her hand on the windowsill.

Adriana screamed again. ''Tis the French!'

Mary glanced outside one more time, hoping her father might be returning at last with some news, but there was nothing. Only the rain, falling harder now, and the boarded-up houses across the plaza.

She pulled the shutters closed and turned back to her maid. The drawing room was usually stylishly grand, with new silk wallpaper and a frescoed ceiling arching high above their heads, gilt-and-satin sofas and chairs clustered around for intimate conversations beside the white marble fireplace. But tonight it was shadowed, echoing, empty.

'Don't be silly, Adriana,' she said again.

'Even General Junot could not cross the Pyrenees so fast as that.'

'But he *is* coming? That is what they say. That Napoleon is angry with Portugal, and is sending his armies. Just as he did in Denmark.' Adriana crossed herself. Everyone knew now what had happened when Napoleon bombarded Copenhagen, punishing them for siding with the British. The port was firebombed and almost a thousand Danish civilians died. No other country wanted such things for their people.

'Of course not. We would have heard something by now,' Mary said. Yet she wasn't so sure. Her father and the rest of the English delegation had been called to the palace complex at Mafra for several days now, trying to persuade the Prince Regent, Dom Joao, to formally ally with the British at last. But Dom Joao was a most indecisive monarch indeed, changing his mind at every moment.

Soon his mind would be made up for him, one way or the other.

'If you go back to England, *senhorita*, you

will take me with you, yes?' Adriana asked
eagerly. 'You would not leave me here?'

'I don't think we will be going back to England any time soon, Adriana. But if we do, I
will take you with me. You don't need to worry
about that,' Mary said with a calm smile. It
would do no one any good to panic now. She
made her way back to her embroidery hoop
by the fire. 'Would you please fetch some tea
now? We should eat something, at least.'

If there was anyone left in the kitchen to
make it for them. Even the Mannings' servants
had been slipping away in the last few days, as
rumours of invasion flew around.

Suddenly, the front door in the hall below
the salon banged open, as if pushed by some
unseen hand. As Adriana sobbed, Mary ran out
to peer over the balustrade, her heart pounding.

It was her father at last, untying his damp
cloak and letting the footman take it. Sir William Manning was generally said, especially
by the ladies, to still be extraordinarily handsome, with his silveri-touched dark hair and
tall figure. But the long days and nights with
the Portuguese court had made his face look

more heavily lined, wearier, his shoulders stooped. She worried that he had no rest of late.

'Papa!' Mary cried, running down the stairs. 'You're here at last. I was getting worried.'

'Mary, my dear.' He kissed her cheek quickly, smiling as if he would try to reassure her. His lips were cold from the rainy night outside. 'You are certainly a sight for sore eyes. Is all well here?'

'Of course. But what of you? What of the royal court?'

He glanced up at where Adriana peered down at them, tears still on her cheeks, her lacy cap crooked. 'Let's go sit down for a while, Mary, just the two of us. Shall we?'

Mary swallowed hard. She knew what it meant when her father needed a quiet word with her. There was news. 'I just sent for some tea. Adriana will fetch it while you warm yourself by the fire. You have been out too long in the chill.'

'We have faced more hardships than a bit of rain, have we not, my dear?' he said wryly, as Mary took his arm and led him up the stairs. Adriana dashed away towards the kitchens.

She settled her father next to the fire, wrapping a fur-trimmed blanket around his shoulders. The wind beat at the shutters, the sky releasing the cold torrents of rain on to the tiled roof. It did sound terribly like guns.

Mary sat on a stool at her father's feet, studying his face carefully. He smiled down at her, but over the years she had learned to look beyond his smile to the worried depths of his eyes.

'Shall we have to face such things again soon?' she asked quietly. 'Has a decisions been made at last?'

He gave a wry laugh. 'I have certainly dealt with my share of ditherers and prevaricators in my work, Mary, as you will know. Everyone is most uncertain when it comes to dealing with Napoleon and who can blame them? But Dom Joao is something else entirely. I do wonder for his sanity. The mother, Queen Maria…'

Mary nodded, thinking of poor Queen Maria, quite mad and shut away in a convent since her husband's death many years before. 'But has he decided?'

'Lord Strangford is a persuasive man, I'll

give him that. I had my doubts when he was appointed to Lisbon.' Lord Strangford, before he was appointed to the Foreign Office, was best known for translating poetry, especially of the Portuguese poet Camões, and was a well-known dandy. But he was also known to be a great defender of British interests everywhere. 'But he has at last shown Dom Joao that time is now of the essence. Junot's Army is making its way towards Lisbon and, when it arrives, they will be no friend to the royal family. It will be too late to flee.'

Mary nodded. She recalled too many stories of what happened to ruling families when Napoleon overran their kingdoms—and of how fast his armies marched. 'He will go, then?'

'And we will go with him. I have my orders from London.'

'When?' Mary asked. She had known this was coming, had prepared for it, but it still made her stomach tighten with uncertainty.

'Very soon, though I have no embarkation dates. Several British warships are on their way to serve as escort across the Atlantic, along with some fresh British diplomats to assist us with the transition. Nothing like this has ever been tried before.' Her father gave a deep sigh and looked into the fire. 'God knows what will happen, my dear.'

Mary nodded, wondering about what might lie ahead—and what Brazil would be like. Not like Russia, of course. And surely not like London, either, which she hadn't seen in so long—and where so many bittersweet memories rested. Brazil would be entirely new. 'It's so far…'

Her father reached down and grasped her hand. 'Too far for you, my dear Mary? We have been in some strange places, true, but nothing like South America.'

Mary squeezed his hand and smiled up at him. 'It will surely be warm there. I would like that after all this chilly rain. South America— it will be quite a grand adventure! I look forward to it.'

She wasn't sure that was *entirely* true. She'd been reading all she could find about Brazil and knew there would be other, not-so-lovely things in addition to the sandy beaches and fresh fruit trees. She read there were few real houses, that there were insects and lizards as large as lapdogs. But it *was* far away. A new beginning, for herself and for her father. Maybe there he could rest.

'Dearest Mary. You are so like your mama. So full of courage and curiosity.' He looked away again, into the fire, and his eyes turned misty, as they always did when he spoke of his wife. Maria Manning had been born in Lisbon, leaving it to marry a handsome young diplomat and journey with him around the Continent. She had been so beautiful, Mary remembered, full of laughter and music. What would her mother think of her homeland now? A mad queen, a prince regent who waffled on every decision, his Spanish wife who loathed him and schemed behind his back. A court that now had to flee across an ocean.

'Would Mama really be excited about seeing Brazil?' Mary asked, hoping to distract her father from his memories and look into the future.

'Of course she would! And what is more, she would be able to persuade everyone else to be excited about it, too. She was a much greater diplomat than I could be.'

'Do some of the royal court still need—persuading? Is there still much reluctance?'

He snorted. 'Reluctant? Ha! If it isn't exactly the way things have been done for five hundred years, these Iberian courtiers won't even consider it. But they'll have to now. It's either go now, or face the French.' His eyes narrowed as he looked down to Mary again. 'Are you still good friends with Doña Teresa Fernandes? The lady-in-waiting to Dom Joao's wife, Doña Carlota?'

'Oh, yes,' Mary answered. 'She is very amusing.' She thought of Doña Teresa, who had stood next to her at one of Mary's first diplomatic receptions in Lisbon and explained who everyone was in wicked, gossipy whispers, with much laughter. Stuffy dinners and balls were always more fun when Teresa was there; she was one of the first friends near her own age Mary had ever met, it made leaving Lady Louisa behind in London a little easier. But she hadn't seen Teresa in several days, everyone had been kept hiding indoors. Doña

Carlota and her court hadn't stirred from their own palace at Queluz.

'Has she said anything about Doña Carlota's views on the embarkation proceedings?'

Mary thought of rumours of Doña Carlota, the Prince Regent's long-estranged wife. She was the daughter of the Spanish King, but had been sent away to marry her cousin when she was only ten years old and was said to have never given up hope she would return to a larger political stage now that her large brood of children were growing. She lived apart from her husband, with her own courtiers, her own schemes. Surely such ambition would follow the Princess across the ocean. 'Just that the Princess has her own—arrangements. She likes having her own court and keeping in contact with her family in Spain.'

'And having her own grand ambitions, I'm sure,' her father said. 'She is certainly a sly one. But she'll have to go to Brazil, too, will she or nil she. I doubt her Spanish family will want the nuisance of her now, they have their own battles to fight. We must preserve British trade with Portugal, especially their South

American holdings, at all costs. You will let me know if you hear anything from Doña Teresa at Queluz?'

Mary only had time to nod as Adriana came in with the tea tray.

'You must eat now, Papa,' Mary said, pouring out a cup of tea and cutting a slice of the almond cake. 'You will need your strength.'

'Yes, and I need sleep, too, I fear. I'm not as young as I once was.' He leaned closer as Mary handed him the cup, and whispered, 'You have been packing?'

She nodded. 'Just as you instructed, Papa. I also burned the papers you had marked.'

'Good girl. I don't know what I would do without you.' He sat back in his chair with a weary sigh. 'You should think of marrying, my dear.'

She gave a startled laugh. Her father had never pressed her on such things, not even when she came home from that ball in London red-eyed and silent. 'Who would I marry?'

'Oh, any number of young men. You would make a perfect diplomat's wife. Or maybe a Portuguese aristocrat? Your mama would have liked that. Doesn't your friend Doña Teresa have a handsome brother all the ladies giggle over?'

'Dom Luis Fernandes. Yes. He *is* rather lovely. Too much for a plain English wren like me,' Mary said, still laughing. She thought of Teresa's brother, his handsome dark eyes and flirtatious ways. He was handsome indeed. And he had never betrayed her trust.

But another face intruded on the thought, an image of brilliant green eyes, and a beautiful smile that had proved so false.

'I shan't marry, Papa,' she said.

'Nonsense! You have your mother's pretty eyes and you are very clever. Much better than all those silly gigglers, eh?'

Mary shook her head. She had certainly not been so 'clever' when it came to Sebastian Barrett. 'Then perhaps I shall find a wealthy planter in Rio de Janeiro, yes? Live my life out in tropical leisure.'

'You laugh, Mary, but you know I'm right. You can't wait on an old man like me for ever.'

Mary swallowed hard. She hated to think of the day when she didn't have her father, didn't have their fascinating, peripatetic life together. 'You said yourself—you can't do without me now. Especially now that we have such a great undertaking as a sea voyage ahead of us.'

'Yes, of course.' Her father wearily closed his eyes. 'A great undertaking indeed...'

Chapter Six

'Shall we avert disaster tonight, do you think?'

Lord Sebastian Barrett glanced across the darkened carriage at his friend Nicholas Warren and laughed. Outside, beyond the curtained windows, he knew the faint lights of Lisbon were falling away as they lurched up into the hills. Rolling meadows and citrus groves, farmhouses and crumbling medieval churches, dashed past, mere shadows in the night as the storm crawled in. But in the carriage, faintly lit by one lamp, was a clutter of letters and diplomatic papers they were supposed to study before they reached the royal palace at Mafra. They had only just arrived and they were being tossed into the maelstrom.

'You and me, Nick?' he scoffed. 'Not bloody likely.'

Sebastian wasn't even entirely sure what he was doing there in Portugal. It had been many months since he left the Army life, a life of long marches and camp life, a hard existence he loved, to take up his late brother Henry's role in the diplomatic corps. *'You must do it,'* his father had raged from his sickbed. *'There have been Barretts controlling the fate of Britain, the power behind the throne, for generations! No more playing soldiers for you. There is real work to be done now'.*

The unspoken words burned in his father's feverish eyes and both Sebastian and the earl knew what they were. *You won't be as good at it as Henry. But you're all there is now. Your older brother must run the estate and he cannot leave the country. But you can.*

So, no—he was not as good at it as Henry. He and Henry had always been the most different of brothers. Sebastian loved his horses, his brandy, pretty women, excitement, danger. Henry was calm, intellectual, methodical. But Sebastian had known his father's words were true. England was balanced on the edge of a stony precipice, with sharks circling below. Many could be soldiers, could take his place in the Army. Fewer could do what a Barrett could do.

So Sebastian had gone through a quick education, learning to do what Henry had been prepared to do—to win England allies to help her stand strong against the might force of Napoleon. Months in Spain and Vienna had sharpened his skills, honed his senses to where he could see what was *not* said, what was only hinted at behind either polite smiles or threatening words.

The skills he had developed over so many card games and drinking bouts where he outlasted his opponents, the ability to read others and make them like him, even against their wills, stood him in good stead now. All those 'deplorable habits' his father once raged against now helped knit England's allies closer to her side as the French tightened their noose around them all. Army life had taught him how to work as a team with others towards a common goal, as well, how to measure his words when needed. How to gauge whether someone was friend or foe.

But still—could Henry have done better? He had done another of his duties to their father when he married the daughter of a viscount and took her with him to Madeira, even though Henry had died soon after the marriage. Their father had tried to get Sebastian to marry a 'suitable' girl as well, had even suggested the sister of Henry's widow. Luckily none of those matchmaking schemes had come off before he had to go to Portugal.

For just an instant, a memory flashed in his mind. A pair of soft, wide grey eyes filling with raw hurt. A small hand turning cold in his, slipping away. Mary Manning turning her back to him when she realised the stark, jagged truth of what he was. A careless rake.

The truth of what he *had* been. Sebastian's fist tightened around the letter he held, crumpling the paper before he even realised it. He was no longer that heedless man. He fought against it every day. Yet remembering Mary Manning, her lovely, heart-shaped face, the way her innocent kiss tasted, made him fight against it all the more. He would never forget the wounded look in her beautiful eyes the last time she had looked at him.

Perhaps his work could now protect more innocents like her. Perhaps, in some small way, he could make amends to her. Not that she would ever know. Surely she was married to some worthy country squire now and never thought of Sebastian at all.

But he thought of *her* all too often.

'Eh, Seb?' Nicholas asked, the tinge of worry in his voice, and Sebastian realised he had been lost in his own thoughts for too long. He tossed aside the crumpled letter and looked across at Nick again.

'What was that, Nick?' Sebastian said.

Nick tried to smile. 'I merely asked if we were going to avert disaster tonight? Or has it already happened?' Like Sebastian, Nick was a more junior member of the Lisbon delegation, though he had been in the diplomatic service longer. In Sebastian's view, there was no one more well-meaning than Nicholas Warren, but also none worse at hiding his own worry.

And when dealing with someone as weak

and indecisive as the Portuguese Prince Regent, worry should never be glimpsed at all.

Sebastian gave Nick his most careless smile. 'I certainly hope so. If the Prince will agree to get himself and his government out of Napoleon's clutches before it's too late, something can be salvaged.'

'And will he?' Nick swallowed hard.

'I certainly hope so. I am rather eager to see Brazil myself. They say there are the most extraordinary dark-eyed women there...'

Nick looked comically shocked. 'Seb! Can you never be serious?'

'Never.' Sebastian knew very well he had to be serious, though no one could see it. People revealed so much more to him if they thought him silly and careless. It had become an unexpected asset.

Thunder crashed down over their carriage, as loud as a cannon shot. The storm that had been threatening ever since they docked at Belem was about to break.

'Here, read these,' Sebastian said, tossing a handful of the documents at Nick. 'We'll be at Mafra soon and Lord Strangford says there's much to be done once we get there.'

Those documents were all from Strangford, the British envoy to Portugal who had been working tirelessly for months to get Prince Joao to formally ally with Britain and embark for Brazil to get out of Napoleon's clutches. Sebastian had been briefed on all that had happened in Lisbon: Joao's dithering, the affairs and machinations of his estranged wife, Doña Carlota of Spain, the English blockades and French threats, and now the fleet that was gathering in the Tagus River to carry them all to the New World.

If Prince Joao could be brought to agree. And he had to agree. *Now.*

Portugal had so far been able to maintain neutrality, but those days were coming to an end. She was hemmed in by Spain, now France's reluctant ally, her warm-water seaport was vital for Atlantic trade and it held as a breach in Napoleon's Continental hold. Strangford was certain this was one of the most important missions of the wars.

At the bottom of one of the letters, the signature was not Strangford's. Sebastian was shocked to see the words *Sir William Manning*.

Mary Manning's father. Sebastian quickly scanned the document, a briefing on a meeting with Joao only the day before, but of course there was nothing about the man's daughter there. Surely she was back in England?

But—what if she was not? What if she was in danger here in Portugal? A rush of protectiveness surged through him, a protectiveness he knew he didn't deserve.

He sat back on the seat as the carriage jolted along the narrow mountain trail. The letter fell from his hand. He looked out the window to see that the palace complex of Mafra, enormous, silent and dark behind impenetrable stone walls, loomed before them. If only he knew where Mary was, could see her again…

'Oh, yes,' he said quietly. 'We shall most assuredly avert disaster here.'

Chapter Seven

Mary was quite sure she had never been to a more dismal ball. She knew she would have to write Louisa of it and tell her that she hoped London balls were more merry.

She stood near one of the tall, brocade-curtained windows of the royal ballroom at the palace of Queluz, studying the scene before her. It was a beautiful room, of course, as all the Portuguese palaces were, lavish and splendid, full of gilded furniture and priceless paintings, marble and gold and scarlet brocade.

And the guests were equally splendid, the ladies in their French fashions of fine muslins and thin silks embroidered with gold and pearls, the hair curled and twined with jewels, the men in their satin breeches and white stockings. Social life at the Braganza court was never exactly sparkling, hampered as it was with elaborate and rigid ritual that was hundreds of years old, as well as fractures in the royal family itself, with Queen Maria mad and her son Dom Joao and his wife, Doña Carlota, estranged. Everyone always took refuge in the latest fashions and in constant whispered gossip.

There were barely even any whispers that night. An orchestra played in their gallery and couples moved across the floor in an elaborate quadrille, but it all had a strangely dreamlike, automatic air. The people clustered around the walls and in the corners stood close together, as if they felt more secure in tight little groups, but they said almost nothing to each other. The only sound was the music, the whisper of silken skirts over the marble floor.

On their gold satin-draped dais at the far end of the room, the Prince Regent Dom Joao and his wife, Doña Carlota, watched the dancing with their oldest children, the royal Princes and Princesses, beside them. The princely couple had long lived apart and only came together for ceremonial occasions, so surely for some reason they deemed tonight to be of some importance. Some unity of the royal family had to be shown in the face of the French threat, of English pressure to flee.

They wore the finest of velvets and satins, yet their faces looked most glum. The royal family were never the prettiest, most jolly of people, but today they looked as if they trudged to their own funerals.

Mary studied the expressions of the people around her, searching for her father. He had brought her to the ballroom, but then he had vanished with Lord Strangford and the others of the English diplomatic group, and she couldn't help but worry about what might be happening.

A cluster of newcomers appeared in the doorway, and Mary glimpsed her friend Teresa Fernandes among them. Teresa was a lady-in-waiting to Doña Carlota, one of the prettiest and most popular ladies at court, and she always seemed to know the latest news. Mary was most happy to see her, to no longer be alone in the crowded ballroom.

After Teresa made her curtsies to the royal couple, Mary found her by the refreshment tables.

'A rather quiet party, isn't it?' Mary whispered as Teresa handed her a glass of punch.

'You should see Her Highness in her own rooms,' Teresa whispered back. 'She paces back and forth, muttering, writing letters to her parents in Spain, then burning them. She does not know what to do.'

'Have you heard anything about the French? About what is happening?'

Teresa shook her head. 'Rumours, of course, but nothing certain. Have you? Has your father said what the negotiations are accomplishing?'

'Not at all. I seldom see him now.' And she worried he had so little rest. Over the rim of her glass, Mary studied the gathering, the dancers who moved through the automatic figures of the stately court dance, the stifling heat from the fires, the crowds in their stiff gowns and satin coats. Everyone's face looked pale, watchful, frightened, no matter how much they tried to pretend this was a normal evening.

The doors at the end of the ballroom opened

and a new group entered. Everyone looked towards them with something like relief, gratitude at the interruption.

Mary hoped it was her father and turned to study the men who waited for the footman to announce them. Suddenly, time seemed to slow and blur, and the crowd vanishing around her. For it was Sebastian Barrett who stood there, the tallest of the group, handsome and watchful in his black-satin court coat.

Mary swallowed hard and looked away for a moment, sure she must be imagining things. But when she turned back, he was still there and it was truly him. He looked startled to see her, as well, and he gave her a bow. Or perhaps it was not even a bow for her.

Mary didn't know where to go, or what to think. It had been so long since she had seen him. She had worked so very hard to forget him and had thought she had mostly succeeded. Now here he was again and she felt just as confused as ever. Just as young and silly.

'I must find my father,' she murmured to Teresa.

'Are you ill, Mary? You look so pale suddenly. Is it this dreadful punch?' Teresa cried. 'Here, let me help you. I need to find the ladies' withdrawing room myself. We can find my brother Luis and have him see us home.'

Mary nodded. She wanted desperately to be out of that overheated ballroom, to be away from Sebastian. She let Teresa take her arm and lead her towards the door, the door which was blessedly empty now. She couldn't see Sebastian and the others, they had vanished into the crowd. She shivered, hot and cold all at the same time.

She and Teresa curtsied hastily to Doña Carlota, who watched them with cold, narrowed dark eyes. Dom Joao leaned over as if to say something to her, but she looked away, smiling at the liveried footman who stood behind her chair.

As Mary turned away, she saw Sebastian waiting to make his bows to the royal couple. But he did not watch them. He watched Mary and a small smile touched his lips.

She hurried away, wishing the marble ballroom floor would open and swallow her whole.

Behind her, she heard a sudden rustle move through the room, across the brocaded and jewelled crowd, and Doña Carlota hurried away from the dais, not even looking at her husband.

Mary wondered if the French were near and her worries about her own heart fled.

It *was* her. Miss Mary Manning.

Sebastian had hoped to catch a glimpse of her there in Lisbon, perhaps even to talk to her again. To make sure she was well, to tell her how he still regretted his youthful folly. To tell her—he wasn't even sure what he would say, what could make it better. He only knew he wanted very much to try.

But now that he really did see her again, he really had no words. All those years of only flirtations had seemingly left him ill prepared for sincerity.

Miss Manning was even lovelier than she had been in London and looked not a day older, even in the stiff formality of the pale-blue satin ballgown trimmed with gold lace, her hair piled high and bound with a lace band. But back then she had a pink glow to her cheeks, a shy smile. Now she seemed pale, solemn, very still and perfectly composed. Her beauty had deepened into that of a woman.

Yet her eyes didn't hold that same light of hopeful innocence that had once drawn him in. He felt a sharp regret, a sudden, burning need to make her smile like that again.

He only had that one look at her, glimpsed through the thick crowd, before she vanished. The ballroom was packed with people in their court satins and velvets, the sparkle of jewels, the faint sound of music, yet no one spoke. They only looked at each other with frightened eyes, moved aimlessly from one group to another.

'This is awfully joyless, eh, Seb?' Nicholas Warren said as he came to Sebastian's side. He took a glass of wine from a waiter's tray, making a face on the first sip. 'I suppose we can't blame them, though.'

'I don't think the Portuguese court has ever been known as an especially mirthful place,' Sebastian answered. 'But now they are faced with leaving their homes…'

Nicholas murmured an agreement. 'At least there are still a few pretty ladies to look at, eh?'

For an instant, Sebastian wondered if Nick had spotted Miss Manning. 'Are there?'

'That one, for instance.'

Sebastian looked towards where Nick gestured with his glass. It wasn't Mary he saw there in the doorway of the ballroom, but one of Doña Carlota's ladies-in-waiting. She was pretty, it was true, and younger than most of the court ladies, with curling dark hair and brown eyes, but she didn't have Mary's delicate sweetness. She went up on tiptoe to whisper to a man beside her, a gentleman just as dark and lithe as she was.

Nicholas sighed and Sebastian laughed at him. But as he started to turn away, another lady joined the pair in the doorway and he realised with a jolt of pleasure that it was indeed Mary. And now she smiled at last—as the dark gentleman bowed over her hand.

Mary laughed at whatever he said to her and Sebastian found himself scowling. He quickly made himself smile again, as he had learned to do so often in the last years, but still he wondered who the blighter was that could make Mary smile.

'Oh, I say—I remember now. Surely that's Doña Teresa Fernandes, whom we met when we presented our credential to the court?' Nicholas said. Before Sebastian could stop him, he made his way across the room to Doña Teresa's side, as unerring on his path as a bee.

Sebastian followed, realising this could be his chance to talk to Mary again at last.

'Ah, Senhor Warren!' Doña Teresa cried, fluttering her lace fan. 'And the Lord Sebastian, yes? It is good to see you again.' Nick bowed over her hand and she laughed. 'Have you met my brother, Dom Luis Fernandes? And my English friend Miss Manning, who I am sure you must already know.'

'I am most honoured to meet you both,' Luis said, with an elaborate, courtly bow. Sebastian realised the man, the one who had made Mary smile, was too damnably handsome. 'You must have come to liven up this dreadful ball, yes?'

As Nick said something, Sebastian realised that Mary watched him, her calm, cool grey gaze never wavering. She did not smile, nor did she frown. He wondered if she even remembered him at all. 'We have met, yes, in England. A long time ago. Lord Sebastian was in the Army then, I remember.'

'So I was,' he answered quietly. 'It is kind of you to recall, Miss Manning. I have long wanted to see you again.'

'Have you?' she murmured.

'What an exciting life it must have been, Lord Sebastian,' Luis Fernandes said. 'You must find Lisbon most dull after the battlefield.'

'I doubt life could ever be dull for Lord Sebastian,' Mary said. 'I do recall many found him most charming indeed in London. Not that everyone would have agreed...'

Sebastian gave her a little bow, as if to acknowledge her small hit. He deserved worse. 'I hope I might be allowed to try to change your mind, Miss Manning.'

'I doubt we will have the time. Or indeed the inclination,' Mary said. With one more cool, sweeping glance over him, she pointedly turned away. 'I think our carriage should be here by now, Teresa? I am quite weary, and must beg to go home.'

'Of course, of course,' Doña Teresa said quickly. 'It *has* been a long evening. Luis, will you see us out?'

'It shall be my great pleasure,' Luis said, offering his arm solicitously to Mary. 'It was a pleasure to meet you, Senhor Warren, Lord Sebastian. I am sure we will see much of you at court now.'

'Perhaps at the next ball!' Teresa said.

'I am sure they will be too busy to dance, Teresa,' Mary said with a smile. With that, she took Luis's arm and strolled out of the ballroom, her shoulders very stiff and straight.

Sebastian watched her go, unable to look away from her. Dom Luis was very solicitous of her indeed, taking her lace shawl from a footman and draping it over her shoulders as she smiled at him. She would surely never deign to smile like that at Sebastian again.

'So that is Sir William Manning's daughter again,' Nicholas said. 'She doesn't seem any fonder of you after all this time, Seb. Not that I can blame her...'

'No, nor can I,' Sebastian answered quietly.

'But you have changed, my friend!' Nick

said with too much heartiness. 'She will come to see that very soon.'

Sebastian tried to laugh, but he feared it came out much too strained. Perhaps he *had* changed—he had grown into himself, into doing his duty. Not that it could make Mary Manning smile at him again.

And his diplomatic skills obviously still needed much honing indeed.

Chapter Eight

It is now. Come at once.

Mary stared down at her father's crumpled note in her gloved hand. Such a small, short thing, delivered by a pageboy who immediately ran off when he thrust it into her hand. But she understood it. It changed everything in a moment. Yet she had been ready. She had been taught to be ready all her life.

The carriage jolted to a halt again, making Adriana wail into her handkerchief. Mary quickly stuffed the note into her reticule, next to her latest letter to Louisa in London trying to explain life in Lisbon, and she peered out the window. What *would* her friend think of such a wild scene?

It was no surprise that the journey from their house to the docks, which would usually take no more than about an hour, was at such a crawling, maddening pace. The maze of alleyways and narrow lanes that wound down from the hills of Lisbon to the river below were crowded with carriages and carts, all piled high with crates and trunks, all inching forward in the churned, sticky mud left by the days of rain. A few brave souls had taken the journey on foot, running past with their belongings balanced on their shoulders, but most of them were trapped in lumbering vehicles.

And time was running out. The British fleet waited to escort the royal convoy out of Lisbon before the French moved in. Mary had to reach them in time.

They inched forward again, and the box Mary held between her booted feet, the box holding their most valuable papers, slid away. She reached down to pull it back and almost hit her head on the cases piled on the opposite seat. Her hat fell down over her eyes, momentarily blinding her. All she had to guide her were Adriana's quiet sobs and the cries and shouts from the street, muffled by the windows.

Mary gave a choked laugh and quickly pressed her hand to her lips to hold it back. There was too much hysteria all around them already. She wouldn't give in to it, too.

She pulled off her hat and tossed it on top of one of the boxes. Adriana sat next to her, Mary's jewel case in her lap, and she looked as pale as milk as she squeezed her eyes shut and whispered a prayer.

'Almost there now, Adriana,' Mary said reassuringly. 'We'll be able to board right away, I'm sure.' She wondered wildly if Sebastian Barrett would be there when she did and how she would feel to see him once more. But there was no time for such thoughts now and she shook them away. But he lingered at the back of her mind. *Damn him.*

Whether they would be able to embark right away was another story altogether. Mary peered outside again, at the slate-grey sky that arched above the tiled roofs and church spires. If it started raining again…

'I hope so, *senhorita*,' Adriana whispered.

'And just think—in a few weeks we shall be in Brazil!' Mary said, determined to stay cheerful. 'I've been reading about it a great deal in the last few days and it sounds most intriguing. It will be winter here very soon, but there it's all golden sunshine and bright blue skies. White sand beaches, which I've never seen before. I'm sure they can't be like the rocky beaches at Dover! And the fruit—I can't wait to taste it. I've never had a mango.'

Mary knew she was babbling, but surely that was better than a heavy, pressing silence where there was nothing to do but think about what was really happening around them—a whole city was fleeing.

It seemed to help. Adriana opened her eyes. 'Mangoes, *senhorita*?'

'Oh, yes. And pineapples. I've lived in many places before, but never anywhere like this,' Mary said. 'I brought my books about Brazil. Perhaps we can read them on the voyage and then it won't seem quite so strange when we get there.'

But it *would* be strange, a hot, tropical place far away from Europe, from everyone they knew. It would be quite intriguing, Mary thought, to have a new start. New friends. A place where no one knew her so very well.

No one like Sebastian Barrett, that was, and he was the very first person she wanted to leave behind. Seeing him at the ball had been too flustering, too overwhelming, and she couldn't afford this kind of distraction now.

The carriage at last reached the docks, but they were caught in a web of all the other vehicles and could go no further. The coachman helped Mary down and, as soon as she stepped out of the carriage, she was consumed in wild noise.

Piled up everywhere were crates stamped with the mark of the royal treasury and the royal library, hundreds of them. Tilted among them haphazardly were pieces of fine, carved furniture from the palaces, and jewelled crosses and plate from churches, all jumbled into boxes. Smaller trunks, cases of linen and provisions of food and wine waited to be loaded as well.

All the carriages had churned deep ruts in the mud and now all was utter chaos. People were screaming, crying, clutching at their belongings. Mary strained up on her toes, but she could see nothing past the press of the crowd that surged around her, the listing stack of crates. She felt carried away by them on a wave of fear and excitement.

She had to find her father, but she saw no familiar faces around her. Many of the ladies wore veils and were swathed in cloaks, but she couldn't glimpse Teresa or any of her other friends. It was just an anonymous sea of humanity, surging around her, carrying her forward.

She hoisted the box of important papers under one arm and grabbed Adriana's hand with the other. 'We must find the *Hibernia*,' she shouted above the roar. That was where her father told her a berth would be waiting; surely if she could just make it aboard, he would rejoin her soon.

But finding her way there seemed a Herculean task. Pulling Adriana with her, Mary pushed her way through the crowd, dodging elbows and snatching hands, ignoring the cacophony of Portuguese and Spanish around her.

'But I have a pass!' one man sobbed, holding up a crumpled, stained paper. He was obviously a court official, with his satin breeches and powdered wig, but he was splashed with mud, like everything around him, and his fine coat was ripped. 'Prince Joao himself promised me a place.'

A soldier pushed him back and Mary slipped past them. The emotion in the heavy, rain-soaked air was so palpable she could almost taste it, sour and metallic at the back of her throat. Frantic fear, desperation, excitement. Children wailed in their nurses' arms, families shouted each other's names. She tried to find her friend Teresa, but couldn't see her anywhere.

Mary swallowed hard to get rid of the fear and pressed onward. Wailing herself would do no good. At last she reached the quay, where rows of skiffs waited to ferry passengers out to the waiting ships. The press of the crowds fell behind her as she tumbled on to the wooden walkway and she faced a most astonishing sight.

Ships as far as she could see, bobbing in the choppy grey waters. Massive, implacable and seemingly so far away. She saw the Portuguese royal flag flying on a few of them, the ships of the line that waited for Dom Joao and his family, and the British colours of their escort. There were many smaller vessels, too, even fishing boats that surely couldn't hope to cross the Atlantic. But everyone was desperate to be gone today, any way they could.

She scanned the galleys and skiffs that were being boarded to row out to the ships, so heavily loaded they rode low in the freezing water, yet she still couldn't see her father. Further down the quay she glimpsed Nicholas Warren from the English delegation, waiting to step into one of the boats.

'Mr Warren!' she shouted in a most unladylike fashion. By some miracle, her words carried above the frantic noise and he turned to wave at her.

'Follow me, Adriana,' she cried, but their path was suddenly blocked by a flock of black-coated officials, all shouting and pushing. She couldn't shove her way through by more than a few inches. She glimpsed the boats rowing out over the water, away from her, and she was trapped in stillness, like in a nightmare.

'Let me help you, Miss Manning,' a deep voice said behind her.

Mary whirled around and was pushed by the pressing crowd into the shelter of a tall, strong body. She knew immediately whose arms closed around her, for surely no one else smelled like that, of a citrus soap and starched linen, even in the midst of mud-splashed chaos. No one else felt like that, of safety and strength. But she knew that safety was just an illusion, for it was Sebastian Barrett who held her.

She wanted to run away, to push him back, to protect herself as she had not been able to in London. But she also wanted to wrap her arms around him and hold on tightly to his strength.

'I…' She tried to step back, out of that confusing warmth of his embrace, but she was trapped against him by the crowd.

'Are you looking for your father?' he asked, his calm tone like an oasis.

Perhaps he was a terrible rake, but he had been blessed with a damnably soothing voice.

Mary tilted back her head to look up at him.

He looked as if he had just stepped into a ball-room, his evening coat sharply tailored and immaculate, his hair falling in bright waves from beneath his hat. She was suddenly pain-fully aware that her own hat was gone, that she was a rumpled mess, her hems splashed with mud, her hair falling from its pins. But this was surely no moment for social niceties.

She forced herself to meet his bright green gaze steadily, to smile. 'Yes. Have you seen him? It took much longer to get here than we planned...' She was shoved again and had to give in and hold on to his arm to keep from falling into the mud. His arm, so warm and strongly muscled, flexed under her touch and his other arm came closer around her.

She glanced back at Adriana, only to find the maid's former fear had fled into fascina-tion with their handsome rescuer. Mary was afraid she looked much the same.

Sebastian looked around them, frowning in concentration, his eyes narrowed. 'That's no surprise, Miss Manning. You're quite fortunate to have made it here at all. I haven't seen your father, but many of the English delegation are engaged in bringing the Prince and his family down to the docks now. Where are you supposed to be?'

'I'm meant to embark on the *Hibernia*, but I'm not even sure how to find it.'

He nodded, and before Mary could know what he intended he bent down and swept her up into his arms. He carried her as easily as if she was a feather and everyone quickly made way for him as he led them through the crowd and deposited her on a seat on the skiff. She dared not even breathe, he was much too close. Several other people crowded on to the small boat, pushing her even nearer to his side.

She tried her hardest to ignore the fact that Sebastian sat so close to her in the small boat, his leg warm against hers through the muslin of her skirts, the velvet of her pelisse. It made her want to stay there for ever, even as she wanted to run away, and she could do neither. At the ball when they first met again, she had been able to run away, but not now.

At last the ship came into view and, despite its formidable, dark hulk against the slate-grey sky, she almost felt relief.

A rope ladder swayed against the side of the ship, sailors peering over the railing high above as the skiff came alongside. One of the rowers leaped out and climbed up the waiting ladder, the wind catching at it with every step. Halfway up, he turned back and held out his hand to help Adriana. Adriana, shrieking and sighing, still found herself able to take the handsome sailor's hand and let him assist her up the side.

Mary had been on voyages before. She jumped up and caught the ladder as Adriana was drawn over the railing on to the deck. But after a few rungs, the heavy wind caught at Mary, catching her breath with its cold touch. The rope was slippery under her gloved hands and her stomach lurched as her whole body swayed. The spray of the waves beneath her made her shiver.

She glanced down and glimpsed Sebastian peering up at her. His face beneath the brim of his hat was dark with—could it be worry? From Sebastian Barrett, charmer of all ladies? Surely not, she thought. The sight of him watching her stiffened her resolve. She wouldn't let *him* see her afraid. See her vulnerable. Not again.

Not ever again.

He looked as if he was about to step on to the ladder, to come after her, and she knew she had to move quickly. She glanced back up and kept climbing. It seemed a mile to the railing and her hands were numb by the time she reached its safety. Two sailors helped her up over on to the deck, as they had with Adriana, and she couldn't seem to stop shivering.

Was it because of the chill—or because Sebastian Barrett was there? Mary found she didn't want to know, not really. He had reappeared so unexpectedly in her life, she was caught completely off-balance. But surely those feelings would pass, as they once had in London.

They *must* pass.

'Oh, *senhorita*!' Adriana cried. She ran forward to wrap a blanket around Mary's shoulders, clucking sympathetic words in Portuguese Mary gave her a grateful smile, tugging the thick wool closer against her, as if it could be armour to the chill both inside and out. She studied the deck around them, waiting as one by one the other passengers from the skiff were bundled on to the deck. It was a crowd of the English citizens who had been living in Lisbon, as well as a few Portuguese aristocrats, sobbing at leaving their home, barely wedged in among crates of papers and boxes stamped with the royal seal. It was crowded, noisy, confusing.

'Miss Manning,' a portly man in a naval uniform liberally laced with decorations called. 'I am Lieutenant Stanhope. Your father asked me to look after you until he arrives. I'm most glad to see you made it safely.'

'Lieutenant Stanhope. How do you do,' Mary said. She glanced over her shoulder to see if Sebastian had arrived on deck, but she couldn't see him yet. She took a deep breath. 'Is my father expected soon?'

'I have had a message that he will make sure the Prince Regent is embarked on the *Principe Real* first, but it should not be long. I have secured a cabin for you and your maid. Rather small, I fear…'

Mary studied the crowded deck again, the

people and luggage piled on every available inch, the snap of the sails overhead. Surely even the tiniest cabin was going to be a rare luxury on this long voyage.

A long voyage where she could run into Sebastian at any moment. Where there would be no place for her to hide her blushes.

'That is most kind of you, Lieutenant Stanhope,' she said, taking a deep breath. She had long learned to never show her real feelings, her real fear.

'Would you care for me to show you the way?' Lieutenant Stanhope asked. He glanced around, wringing his gloved hands together, and Mary knew he was very busy indeed.

'I think I will keep watch here on deck for a bit longer, thank you. If I won't be in the way here,' she said.

'Not at all. If you will just excuse me...'

As the captain hurried away, the last of the passengers, already dazed by the rough waters and the cold wind, landed on the deck. Sebastian was the last to appear.

He looked at Mary again, with that solemn, searching expression on his face. She couldn't fathom what he wanted from her, what he thought when he watched her. To make fun of her again? To hurt her? She was not the lonely girl she had been then; she wouldn't fall for that charm again.

She turned sharply away from him, from that sea-green gaze that seemed to see far too much, and hurried to a slightly quieter spot by the rail, where she could watch for her father.

From that distance, the chaos at the docks looked far removed, rather like the scurrying of a hive of bees. More carriages had arrived, getting lodged in the mud, and crates and trunks were growing in tottering piles as their owners ran between them. But Mary knew all too well the full seriousness of what she watched. A whole empire was being tumbled about, to land wherever they might, and the whole Continent would never be the same.

She peered across the bay at the Portuguese royal vessels, the ship of the line the *Principe Real*, meant to carry Dom Joao and his heir, and the others prepared for his wife, Doña Carlota, and all their royal relatives—if they appeared. She saw no signs of them yet, only the courtiers trying to find their own berths however they could.

She shivered again and drew the blanket closer around her.

'Mary! Is it truly you? Oh, how glad I am to see a face I know!'

Mary spun around to see her friend Teresa running towards her across the crowded deck. Her usually impeccably fashionable appearance was rumpled, her black hair tumbling from its pins, a shawl wrapped around her shoulders as meagre protection against the cold. She dodged around aimlessly milling passengers, waving her hands above her head.

'Teresa! I was worried about you,' Mary cried as Teresa threw her arms around her. Mary, too, was overjoyed to see a familiar face, to know a friend was there amid the chaos. 'How did you get on the *Hibernia*?'

'A stroke of only luck, I fear,' Teresa said. 'Luis got us passes from Dom Joao for berths on the *Alfonso de Albuquerque*, with my mistress, Doña Carlota, but when we arrived at the docks we could make no one hear us. Such appalling treatment! Can you imagine?'

Mary thought of the man in the crooked wig and torn knee breeches, arguing that he had a pass. 'I fear I can imagine all too well after what I've seen today. The docks are crowded with people desperate to get away. But thankfully you are here now and can share my cabin.'

Teresa shuddered. She wore only a thin muslin gown and silk spencer jacket with her shawl. Mary quickly wrapped her own blanket around her friend's shoulders. 'I have never imagined anything like it. My aunt, who was a nun, would have said it was the end of days. But *you* saved us, my friend!'

'Me?' Mary said in disbelief.

'Of course. I saw a man in one of your English naval uniforms and I told him I knew you and your father. He made sure we were loaded into a skiff that was just leaving, and here we are, safely away.'

'We?'

'Luis, of course. He pushed our way through that fearful crowd.' Teresa peered over Mary's shoulder at the crowd around them and waved.

Mary glanced back to see Teresa's brother

making his way towards them. He was so tall and dark, so dashing, that ladies all around the deck stopped to peek at him, despite the fearful circumstances.

'Miss Manning! Our heroine.' He dramatically caught up her hand and bowed over it, making her laugh. She saw why all Lisbon was so charmed by the Fernandes siblings; they made her forget even her own worries, if only for a moment. 'Teresa was most clever to use your name. Surely you can open all doors in this English world.'

Mary laughed. 'Not all, I fear.' She couldn't solve her own lingering feelings for Sebastian Barrett, though she was determined she *would* conquer it, one way or another. 'But I am glad I could help you make it here safely, even if only in a very small way.'

'Not small at all.' He kissed her hand again and Mary suddenly glimpsed Sebastian further along the rail, watching her and Luis. She couldn't read his expression at all.

Mr Nicholas Warren appeared at Luis's shoulder, blocking Mary's glimpse of Sebastian. She smiled at him, grateful for the distraction.

'Miss Manning!' Mr Warren cried. 'You arrived safely after all, thank goodness.'

'And you, Mr Warren. Everything does seem most uncertain today,' Mary answered, carefully sliding her hand out of Luis's. She smiled politely at Mr Warren, even as she still remembered all too well he had been one of Sebastian's wild friends in London. 'Do you remember my friend, Doña Teresa Fernandes, and her brother, Dom Luis? I believe you met at the Regent's ball. This is Mr Nicholas Warren, a member of the English delegation with my father. It seems we are to travel together.'

Mr Warren turned to Teresa—and his bluff, handsome face reddened, as so many men's did when faced with Teresa's Portuguese beauty. He gave a hasty bow. 'I haven't—that is, I am most happy to have the pleasure again, Doña Teresa,' he stammered.

Teresa offered him her hand with a bright smile, as if she was in a ballroom and not on the deck of a chaotic ship. Mary couldn't help but admire such sang-froid. 'I am sorry our meeting must be under such trying circumstances, Mr Warren. I fear I am not at my best.'

'I think then I should be most nervous to see what your best could be, Doña Teresa,' he said with a nervous laugh. 'It must be quite fearsome.'

'They are here! The royal family has arrived!' The cry flew along the deck like a rush of cold wind. Mary was suddenly jostled, pushed up close to the rail as everyone strained for a glimpse of Dom Joao and his family, on whom this whole enormous risk rested.

Mary held up her hand against the grey glare of the light, but all she could see was a line of large, luxurious carriages lumbering towards the docks, jostled on all sides by the desperate crowds still ashore.

Suddenly the danger, the running out of precious time, seemed all too real.

She felt a warm touch on her arm and glanced up to see Sebastian had somehow made his way to her side. His face was still expressionless, his eyes such a dark green as he looked down at her. He silently held out to her a telescope. She slowly accepted it, unsure, but strangely hopeful.

She turned away, all too aware of him standing close to her, as he had on the skiff. The scent of him seemed to wrap around her on the cold breeze and it steadied her. She lifted the telescope and studied the scene on shore, suddenly amplified through the tiny glass.

It looked even more wild than before, a swarm of people whose desperation was palpable even across the turbulent waves. The skies overhead were filling with swirling clouds and the ships rode low, as if becoming dangerously overloaded. No one wanted to be left behind, especially now as the moments flew by.

Even Mary had been unable to fully realise the magnitude of what was happening, after all she had seen in her travels with her father, all she had heard in the last few days about Napoleon's armies creeping closer. Now here were the royal carriages. They were truly going.

Mary remembered royal ceremonies she had attended in the past, the gold and velvet, the music and the canopies of state, the great processions. There was none of that now. Now, as she watched through Sebastian's telescope, the black carriages, marked with the Braganza arms on the doors, lurched to a halt next to a mere gangway lodged in the mud that led to a large skiff.

With no fanfare at all, the portly figure of Dom Joao emerged, wrapped in a cloak, followed by his son, the lanky Prince Pedro Carlos, and a few servants. They were hastily bundled into the boat, surrounded by British officers.

A procession of courtiers followed, servants carrying little princes and princesses, elderly royal aunts blinking in the light as if still bewildered and the Prince's wife, Doña Carlota. She was still as short and stout as ever, wrapped in a bright red cloak, her head crowned with a yellow-satin turban that made her stand out from the others, much more grandly dressed than her husband. She stopped and looked around as if she expected more ceremony, but none was forthcoming, even for her.

Like her husband, she was carried on to a boat and hastily rowed out to the Portuguese ships that awaited them.

'I hope they don't put the Prince and his wife on the same vessel,' Mr Warren commented. 'Their quarrels will swamp everyone before they even reach Madeira!'

'Senhor Warren!' Teresa cried. 'How dare you?'

'Senhorita Fernandes is lady-in-waiting to Doña Carlota,' Mary said quietly, still watching as one last carriage arrived, buffeted on all sides by the crowds.

'Oh!' Mr Warren gasped. 'I do apologise, Senhorita Fernandes. I meant no disrespect at all.'

Teresa laughed. 'I am sure you say nothing everyone else merely thinks. My mistress is not—fond of her husband.'

'I believe Doña Carlota is to be aboard the *Albuquerque* with two of her daughters,' Sebastian said. 'I think she will not see the Prince Regent until we arrive in Salvador.'

Mary still watched the last carriage, trying to stop herself from being pushed against Sebastian. No one at first emerged as the carriage doors were opened and she sensed the breathless tension as everyone waited to see what would happen now. It was like a particularly unpredictable play, one where anything at all could happen at any moment.

For a moment, she could see little but the swirling grey and black of the crowd on the docks. At last a man in the ornate livery of the Braganza family, all blue and gold in the gloom, reached inside the carriage and pulled out a tiny, struggling white-haired woman in a black gown and mantilla.

'Queen Maria,' Teresa said in a stunned whisper.

It was indeed the Mad Queen, fighting at every step. At last she was loaded into a boat with her attendants and the royal family was all gone from the shore.

Mary lowered the telescope, holding her breath. Sebastian still stood beside her and she hated to admit the feeling of security it gave her to know he was there. If *he* was the only safety in the world now, things were topsy-turvy indeed.

'We shall not weigh anchor until the morning tide, I would think,' Stanhope said, studying the clouds swirling overhead. 'If the weather holds, that is. Ladies, would you prefer to wait in your cabin? It will be a bit warmer there.' He was all politeness, but Mary could tell he wanted them out of the way of the business that had to be done to get them out of Lisbon.

'Oh, yes, thank you,' Teresa said with one of her bright smiles. She briefly rested her hand on the lieutenant's sleeve and Mary couldn't help but notice how Mr Warren was watching, his face growing red again. Teresa did have that effect on men.

But not, it seemed, on Sebastian Barrett. He still watched Mary and she turned away, flustered.

'I shall wait just a little longer for my father,' Mary said. 'But you go ahead, Teresa. I will meet you there soon.'

'Surely it is too cold to wait on deck, Miss Manning,' Sebastian said. 'You could catch a chill.'

Was that concern he tried to put into his tone? Mary whirled around to face him, afraid she was all too prone to falling for that, for *him*, all over again if she was not careful. But surely she was not that silly girl she had been in London now. 'You can have no concern as to whether I am too cold or not, really, Lord Sebastian. You must have far more important concerns to occupy you at the present.'

His jaw tightened. 'Miss Manning. I only wish for your comfort.'

He had not cared at all for her 'comfort' in London and she shivered as she remembered how foolishly hurt she had once been to learn that. She glared up at him and he frowned as he looked back at her. They seemed bound in an instant of silence, amid all the tumult around them, and she found she couldn't break away.

'I can stay with Miss Manning until her father arrives,' Luis said smoothly, sliding next to Mary to lay his hand on her arm. He smiled politely at Sebastian.

Mary felt her cheeks turn warm, despite the cold breeze, and was deeply disconcerted to find that Sebastian Barrett could still affect her thus. She turned back to the railing and stared down at the swirling grey water far below.

'Thank you, Senhor Fernandes,' she murmured. From the corner of her eye, she saw Sebastian give a small bow before he strode away with some of the officers. Mr Warren led Teresa off towards their cabin and for a moment Mary felt very alone there at the ship's railing.

'I have heard great tales of Brazil,' Luis said. 'That there is sun every day and coconuts as big as man's head falling straight off trees. Ocean water as warm as a bath and music everywhere.'

Mary could tell he was trying to distract her and she was grateful. He was so handsome and charming, every lady in Lisbon seemed half in love with Luis Fernandes, and the fact that he would take time to talk to his sister's friend was kind.

If only he could make her forget Sebastian was out there some place.

But her gratefulness almost evaporated at his next question.

'Do you know this Senhor Lord Sebastian Barrett, then?' Luis asked and Mary could feel him watching her closely. 'Were you perhaps friends back in England?'

Mary could not fathom why he would ask that. Had she revealed some of her emotions without realising it? Why would Luis even be interested? 'I met him once or twice in London, when he was still serving in the Army. I was rather surprised he is now with the Foreign Office, but I do think the Barretts have long served in diplomatic positions.'

'And do you like him? All the ladies seem to. And he seems to know much about the affairs of Iberian politics.'

Mary made herself laugh and she was afraid it sounded rather harsh. 'I should think that would be his job now. But I confess I do not care for him very much. His manners are not— all they should be.'

Luis suddenly reached for her hand and she looked up at him in surprise. In the flickering light of the ship's lanterns, his lean, dark, handsome face, usually as merry as his sister's, was so very serious. He looked deep into her eyes and she had to turn away, flustered.

'Senhorita Manning,' he said quietly. 'No man should ever treat you with anything less than worship. This Lord Sebastian is foolish indeed if he has made you dislike him.'

Flustered, Mary drew away her hand. 'Senhor Fernandes, I—that is, I think…'

The sudden movement of a boat breaking through the water below caught her attention. She turned towards it, grateful for the distraction. It seemed she had learned little in dealing with men's attentions since Sebastian in London and she felt rather silly. Silly and unsure.

Much to her relief, one of the men in the crowded vessel was her father.

'Papa!' she cried, waving. He glanced up, and a smile broke across his worried face under the brim of his hat.

'Mary, my dear,' he called back. 'Thank heaven you got away in time.'

Got away. Mary thought of Sebastian Barrett, his arms around her as he swung her up off her feet and into safety. She was suddenly afraid she had run away from Napoleon, only to fall into other trouble. Trouble for her uncertain heart.

Chapter Nine

'Whatever shall happen to us, Mary?' Teresa whispered. She pulled the blankets of the berth up over her head, but Mary could still hear her friend's muffled sobs.

'We shall move through this, of course, and see sun tomorrow,' Mary answered, though in truth she wasn't entirely sure. When the fleet slipped past the bar amid deafening cannon salutes, moving into open sea, they had immediately been buffeted by gale winds, which hadn't yet ceased. The ships had tacked off their course, drawing in their sails, trying to avoid the worst of the storm and move in safety further into the Atlantic and on the way to Brazil.

Mary had travelled much in her life, but

the howling of the wind, the wooden crashes overhead and the loud sobs of the passengers crowded around them in the other cabins was unlike anything she had experienced. She was trying to write it all down in her letter to Louisa, which seemed to have become a way of making sense of it herself.

'Do you truly think so?' Teresa said.

'Of course. I should go see if I can find some tea, or even a bit of brandy. That will settle our stomachs and I can find out what is happening as well.'

'I should fetch that, *senhorita*. It is my job,' Adriana said weakly from her berth tucked under the tiny porthole. Ever since Mary had taken her aboard, away from the chaos of Adriana's home city, the maid had been even more eager to help. But her face was an alarming greyish-green colour and Mary feared she would be too weak.

'No, you both stay here and rest, my stomach is quite made of iron,' Mary said quickly, tucking away her letter. 'Read some of the books on Brazil. I won't be gone long.'

Wrapping her cloak around her, she hurried

out of the cabin and carefully shut the door behind her, so it would not bang open every time the ship rolled. The corridor was narrow and dark, pitching under her feet as the wind tossed them around. Behind the other doors, she heard muffled sobs and voices, moans and then the unmistakable sour smell of seasickness.

She peeked into the small cabin assigned to her father, but he was not there, and she feared he was still working far too hard.

The *Hibernia* was a large warship, but she was crowded to the rafters with passengers. Mostly British citizens who had been living in Portugal, merchants and diplomatic families like Mary's, and a few Portuguese aristocrats who hadn't been able to lodge anywhere else. It was a bad start to a very long voyage, all stormy upheaval, and she could feel the fear and misery pressing around her, like a physical thing that tried to push her down.

But Mary didn't want to be held down. Holding on to the wooden wall, she carefully made her way to the steep stairs at the end of the corridor. A rope banister was strung along there and she used it to pull herself up on to the deck.

A cold wind bit into her cheeks and tugged her hair from its pins, reviving her. The salty spray, even chilly as it was, felt fresh after the stale, sour air below decks and she welcomed it even as the scene that greeted her was a frantic one.

The top sections of the masts had been dismantled and lashed down, she saw at a quick glance, and sailors rushed around everywhere, a melee of running feet and shouts. A few passengers were huddled together near the railings, their faces pale and terrified in the swaying lamplight. They seemed to be straining for one last glimpse of their home, but Lisbon was left far behind in the fog.

Mary wrapped her cloak closer around her and found a quiet spot at the railing, out of the way of the crew. She studied the scene in front of her, but all she could see was a blur of black and grey. Waves crashed against the ship's hull and clouds whirled past overhead. In the distance, she could barely make out the outlines of the other vessels, tossed like their own by the wind. The creak and moan of straining wood crashed through the air.

They were like toys, she thought, tiny, delicate things cast adrift in an unfathomable, vast sea. But Mary had felt like that for most of her life, tossed into situations she only half-understood in her father's political life, and was expected to grope her way through. A stormy ocean was surely just another challenge.

Only once, for a few precious days, had she begun to feel like there was an anchor cast her way that she might be able to grasp. When she had first met Sebastian Barrett in London and new, bright feelings had left her so uncertain and delighted.

But that had all proved to be the most unpredictable storm of all. She was not going to do that again, leave herself so vulnerable to emotions.

Mary held on tightly to the railing, the polished wood slick and cold under her hands. She stared out at the white, frothy waves, whipped higher and higher around them, but she didn't really see them. She saw Sebastian as he had been as he stood next to her as Lisbon fell away before them. The way he looked at her, so unreadable and—and maddening.

Once she had let herself cease to be cautious, had been young and foolish, and opened her thoughts and feelings to him. Even now, knowing what she did about him, she found herself intrigued by him all over again.

Damn him. He upset the careful, content inner world she had managed to build for herself, a world where she could be useful. If she sometimes, very late at night, felt some pang of unspoken longing—well, she knew it would quickly pass, lost in work. Usually.

But Sebastian Barrett was like this storm, unpredictable, frightening and yet somehow alluring in its very changeable nature. Just by his very presence he unsettled her. He always seemed to be there when she was at her most awkward, to catch her as she fell.

'I won't allow it,' Mary whispered fiercely. She slapped her palm down hard on the railing—and felt her feet slip away underneath her on the wet planks of the deck. A rush of panic caught her in its cold grip.

A hard, strong arm came around her waist, lifting her up before she could crack her head on the railing. She was swept up to safety again, the wind catching at her.

'May I help?' a deep voice said near her ear, a voice that was all too familiar. It made her shiver with its heat.

Blast! It was Sebastian, of course. Her thoughts of him seemed to conjure his very presence all the time now, especially when she seemed to be at her most awkward worst—like on the docks, and like now.

Yet she couldn't honestly say she wished he hadn't appeared, that he had let her topple into the cold water so far below. Or that his touch was—unpleasant. Yet it was certainly most unsettling.

'Th-thank you,' she said. 'I should be more careful.'

'Indeed you should, Miss Manning.' He still held her tightly against him, blocking the wind like he was a haven from the storm itself. 'A ship's deck in a storm is no place to be wandering about.'

'I'm not the only passenger outside now,'

she protested, all too aware he still held her—and that she didn't really want him to let go. 'I couldn't bear to be trapped in that cabin for a moment longer.'

'I can't blame you for that. It's a miserable situation.' He carefully set her on her feet at last, her body slowly sliding along his.

She spun around to face him. She stepped back so quickly, he had to grab her arm to steady her.

'I thought you were once in the Army, not the Navy,' she said. She heard herself and feared her tone was far more accusing than she meant it to be. He still made her feel so young and uncertain—so foolish.

He smiled at her, so full of life and golden beauty that, for a moment she couldn't breathe. 'I am following in my family's footsteps now, just as you are. We must do our best for our country now, yes?'

'I—yes, of course,' Mary murmured. Could he truly have changed in the last two years, following a path not of his own making? Was the new solemnity in his eyes real? She didn't know what to trust.

The boat lurched on the waves, sending her off balance. His arms suddenly came around her again, tugging her closer. Mary clutched at his shoulders to hold herself upright and she found she couldn't move away. It felt like it had in London, so intoxicating and irresistible.

The cold wind twined around them, whipping her cloak around them both, as if to bind them together in that strange, dreamlike twilight world.

'We must beware the storms of the world, Mary,' he whispered warmly against her ear.

It still seemed as if she was caught in a dream, yet at the same time it was more real than anything she had ever known, when his head dipped down towards her and he kissed her.

The touch of his lips was so soft at first, warm, enticing, pressing to hers teasingly once, twice. It felt so strange, and yet so familiar, too, this kiss that had haunted her dreams since they last met. When she didn't, couldn't, move away, when her hands tightened on his shoulders, his kiss deepened. It became hotter, more urgent, as if he felt drawn into that desperate unreality, too. She needed to feel alive again and he was the only thing that made her so.

She moaned, parting her lips until she felt the tip of his tongue slide against hers, seeking entrance. The whole unsure world around them vanished and there was only *him*. Only the way he made her feel, completely outside of herself.

It was a delirious moment that shattered all too soon. A shout, and a resounding wooden crash, broke into her instance of insanity. She tore her mouth from his, tilting her head back to suck in the cold, thought-clearing air.

He, too, stepped away, his broad shoulders heaving on a deep breath. For just a moment, his unreadable mask had fallen and she saw a flash of raw passion in his eyes. A passion that answered hers. But then it was gone, vanished into another expression she knew all too well—remorse.

'Mary, I must…' he began hoarsely.

'No,' she whispered. No words could erase the hurts of the past, or the confusion of the present. No words could explain what she was feeling, even to herself. She only knew she couldn't bear it if he was *sorry.* 'I must go.'

She spun around and dashed across the slippery deck as fast as her boots could take her.

What was he thinking, to dare to kiss Mary like that?

But Sebastian feared he knew—he had not been thinking at all. Not in that moment, with the wild seas beyond them, and Mary looking up at him with her wide grey eyes. He had lost control, in a way he had hoped was left far behind him. He had even hoped he might prove to Mary he had changed, only to toss it all away as if he had heaved it overboard into the ocean.

And yet—yet her lips had tasted so very sweet, almost as if he'd been dying of thirst until he touched her again.

He leaned against the railing as he raked his hand through his hair. He was glad of the cold wind, of the stark reminder of where they were, who they were. He couldn't forget again.

Not if he was truly to gain her forgiveness.

Chapter Ten

'If the weather improves, we should be in Madeira in only a few more days,' the captain announced as he passed an ewer of wine around the dinner table in his spacious cabin.

Mary smiled as she took a little more of the wine. Everyone aboard had been speaking of 'better weather' ever since they pushed out of the Tagus and into open sea. The unrelenting winds kept buffeting them across the choppy waves and the damp, dark grey fog out of sight of the other ships. It felt as if they floated in their own world, cut off from all other people, all news, all sunlight.

That wasn't quite true, of course. Mary had stood at the railings and watched boats being lowered, carrying messengers to the royal vessels, assessing damage and levels of supplies, even transferring passengers when needed. It was a whole floating wooden world out there.

Mary was one of the few not yet laid low by seasickness. During the day, she helped nursing other passengers, bringing broth and wine and clean basins, talking to the sailors who had made this journey many times and had tales to tell of the islands and of Brazil itself. Her father was always busy with his meetings, hidden away in the captain's cabin with the other men of the diplomatic party, and she seldom saw him except at dinner.

But she also seldom saw Sebastian, which she was grateful for. After their kiss, she didn't know what to say to him, how to behave—how to hide from him so she could not be hurt by him all over again.

That didn't keep him from her thoughts, though. Especially at night, when she couldn't sleep. She would lie in her berth, listening to Teresa and Adriana in their restless slumber, and would remember London, her foolish young infatuation for him, the way he looked different now. What had happened to him since they parted?

She feared she was being fooled by his charm all over again.

Mary took a sip of the wine, wishing it could fortify her against herself. She had deluded herself for so long, thinking she had outgrown the silly girl who was so infatuated with Sebastian Barrett. Yet she feared she hadn't really changed at all, as he seemed to have done.

Her fingers tightening around the stem of her glass, she frowned down into the red depths. Of course she had changed. She could see now how foolish she was, where then she had leaped ahead, so sure Sebastian was a fairy tale come true. But there were no fairy tales, not in real life. There was only war and people who had to flee their homes, and love gone badly.

She peeked over the rim of her glass at where he sat at the other end of the tables, talking to Mr Warren and one of the ship's officers. He was still handsome, perhaps even more than he had been back then, with a new darkness in his eyes. He looked at her and she turned away, flustered.

It was a small group at dinner, thanks to the pitching waves. The captain and his officers, Mary's father and his secretaries, Sebastian and Mr Warren. The only other ladies were a stout Portuguese countess, who talked about the villa on the beach she intended to have in Brazil, and Teresa, who had pulled herself out of bed to come to the table and flirt with Mr Warren.

'But I understand you intend to leave us before Madeira, Lord Sebastian,' the captain said.

Startled, Mary looked back towards Sebastian. Leave them? She felt a sudden jolt of something that felt oddly like relief—and dismay.

'Yes, that is true,' Sebastian said with a smile. The Portuguese countess sighed. 'I fear Mr Warren and myself have orders to transfer to the *Reina de Portugal* to oversee the voyage with the Prince Regent. We are to transfer by skiff as soon as possible.'

'Better you than me,' the captain said, laughing. 'That ship seemed to be in poor shape before we even left Lisbon. If you reach Rio long after we do…'

The conversation went on around her, but Mary did not really hear it. She sipped at her wine and secretly studied Sebastian in the candlelight. She did not know if she was glad he was going to be on another ship for their long journey, or if she was sorry they couldn't speak together more. That she couldn't find out what had truly happened between them in London.

After the meal, she made her way out to the deck to watch as the skiffs were lowered for the journey to the *Reina de Portugal*. It was a chilly night, a cold wind sweeping up from the sea, the waters below sprinkled with lights from the stars. She wrapped her shawl closer around her, listening to the echo of chatter from the cabins beyond. It was a strange night, lonely and beautiful.

She drew back into the shadows as Sebastian and Mr Warren made their way to the railing, their tall figures wrapped in greatcoats. Sebastian glanced back and for an instant Mary was sure he saw her standing there.

She shrank back, hardly able to breathe, but in the next moment, he was gone from her sight.

She was alone in the night.

Chapter Eleven

Seven weeks later

'Land! Land!'

The shout echoed from the deck above, through the open porthole to where Mary and Teresa were playing a lazy game of cards in their cabin. They glanced at each other and then leaped to their feet to race down the corridor, Adriana close behind them with her mending still in her hand.

The deck was already crowded, everyone pushed out of their long doldrums, the long, slow days, by that wondrous word—*land*. It had been weeks since they had seen anything but endless grey waves, the other ships in the royal convoys mere specks in the distance.

While they certainly didn't suffer from the privations some of the other vessels were said to endure—lice that forced Doña Carlota and her ladies to shave their heads; no food but salted fish and ship's biscuits; low levels of fresh water—life on the *Hibernia* had become dull, but not difficult.

And now the journey seemed near to being over.

The long, lazy days of reading and cards with Teresa and Adriana, while her father was closeted with the other diplomats, had left Mary far too much time to think about Sebastian Barrett. Since he had transferred to another vessel, she had learned nothing of him and it seemed to make her think of him even more.

Made her remember the ways he had seemed changed in Lisbon, the new solemnity in his eyes, the watchful way he seemed to observe everything around him. The way he watched *her*. She was so unsure of him, so wary of trusting any changes. Wary of *him*.

What would happen when she saw him again?

She and Teresa found a small space between the crowd at the rail and she shielded her eyes from the golden sunlight in the endless stretch of pale-blue sky overhead. For days, it had been growing warmer and warmer, the air softer. After the grey chill of the onset of a Portuguese winter, the light was intense, unyielding.

Mary peered closer. Without a glass, the shore of Brazil seemed to be a mere dark ripple in the distance, a tiny break in the endless expanse of sea and sky. It almost seemed like a dream.

But the bustle and noise of the crew was real enough. Once the storms of their departure from Europe were past, the voyage since Madeira had been a blessedly quiet one. Perhaps *too* quiet at times, such as when they drifted for a few days, becalmed in the middle of the Atlantic, but even the sailors had become lazy. They danced in the evenings with passengers, told tales of other, more perilous voyages. Now they were suddenly scaling the masts, letting the sails billow free to carry them to their destination.

The shore grew closer and closer. Mary could make out a crescent-shaped sweep of pale golden beach. Dark, shining volcanic rock shapes rose up out of the bright blue water like sea creatures. The famous Sugarloaf Mountain was off to the side, leaning back as if it was a guard at the entrance to the city. In the distance were great, dark mountains, looming all around, almost cutting into the fluffy white clouds.

Between the bay and the mountains she could see the city, white walls winding up the hillsides, much like Lisbon had been, all washed in that vivid, wondrous light.

What would she find there? Mary sensed a whole new voyage just beginning in those mysterious new streets, a world she couldn't even yet fathom despite all her reading. Maybe she could even make herself into something new!

Something that wouldn't be unsure of seeing Sebastian Barrett again, that would laugh at him and all he had once made her feel.

'Mary!' she heard her father call. She glanced over her shoulder to see him hurrying across the crowded deck. He took her hand tightly in his as he stared out at the bay, at the other ships drawing closer. Mary feared he looked tired, his eyes darkly circled with worry. She hoped the sun might help him, too. That here, so far from the troubles in Europe, he could get some much-needed rest.

He gave her a smile. 'Soon, my dear Mary, we'll have solid ground under our feet again at last, eh? Maybe this time we will stay put for a while.'

'I can't wait to see Rio, Papa,' Mary said, trying to give him a reassuring smile in return. 'And you will have plenty of fresh fruit to eat, and time to rest.'

He laughed. 'No time to rest now, my dear. I think the real work is just starting. But I do have my Mary to help me.'

'Of course, Papa,' she answered, thinking of her beautiful mother and how Maria always was there for her husband and child. Of how family was the only real home, the only really important thing. 'You'll always have me to help you.'

He gave her a mock-severe frown. 'Not *al-*

ways, I hope. Lovely young ladies like my Mary need their own families.'

Before Mary could answer, there was a sudden booming salute from the cannons lined up along the docks. She looked up, startled, to see that the royal ships had drawn closer in the harbour as they approached the shore. She could make out figures now, people lining the wharf as they waited to welcome their royal family from across the ocean. Mary couldn't help thinking it must be rather like meeting mythological figures, suddenly stepping down from a painting.

She glimpsed a skiff making its way across the choppy white waves. The figure seated in the prow wore the blue sash of a lord mayor, and Mary thought it must be Lord Arcos, the viceroy of Brazil, who had been given only a few weeks to prepare for this most momentous of events. As he drew near the ships, there was the muffled sound of cannon fire out over the water. The acrid scent of smoke combined with the sweetness of the blossoming orange groves on shore, and the salty sea breezes.

'So we are safe here from that devil Napoleon,' Teresa said.

Mary glanced at her friend, startled by the sudden, serious sound of Teresa's voice.

'Yes,' Mary answered. 'But not from other things?'

Teresa laughed. 'We are never safe from *all* things, *minha amiga*. But I suppose we will be able to make merry here. And I will serve Doña Carlota again, so I am sure there will be balls and dinners, just like at home. Will the officers be as handsome after such a long voyage, do you think?' She tossed Mary a teasing look, making them both laugh. 'Not as handsome as my brother. So many ladies are so fond of him, but he has spent much time with us lately. I doubt it is *my* company he likes so much.'

'I am sure I don't know what you mean, Teresa,' Mary said. She turned away to look at the beach again, feeling her cheeks turn warm. Luis Fernandes *had* dined with them often in the voyage, always laughing, always entertaining them. Luckily he had not said anything else like his words in Lisbon. She didn't know what she would say to him if he did. She liked him very much, of course, but....

But he was not like her old dreams of Sebastian Barrett and those had to be banished.

There, on the wharfs, were the English diplomats who had been sent ahead on a faster boat, a collection of sombre dark coats against the vivid green and white of the shore. Was Sebastian among them? She was sure he was. But she didn't know yet how she would react to seeing him again.

She only knew she had to figure it out very soon indeed.

Chapter Twelve

Mary opened the shutters of her new sitting room, letting the brilliant sun cascade inside. It made the layer of dust over everything visible, tiny flakes of silver dancing in the warm, stuffy air, but it also showed her details of this new home she hadn't been able to fully see when they arrived late the night before.

They had been brought ashore while the fireworks still exploded in the night sky over the royal ships, so her father could help oversee preparations for the Braganzas to disembark, all the elaborate ceremonies the colonial crowds would expect. Mary had seen little of the city in the dusk, aside from bumpy, dusty roads, the shimmer of mysterious light behind lacy, latticework balconies, the enticing scent of flowers on the breeze, the heat of the day still caught in the darkness. The feelings of it were so intriguing and she couldn't wait to see more.

For now, though, there was just the small house they had been given off the main square of the city. The morning light was brilliant, piercingly golden and clear, unlike any she had ever seen before. She had lived in so very many places with her father over the years, Mary thought as she studied the room, but nothing like Brazil.

The house was a simple one, with white-plastered walls, tall, beam-crossed ceilings and heavy, dark carved furniture that looked almost medieval. Old, silvery mirrors framed in curlicues of gilt hung high on the walls. Soon, she knew, it would be her own, once their crates were opened and she could unpack their own silver and china, the porcelain orna-ments they had found in Russia, her mother's portrait and some lighter curtains at the win-dows. It would seem as much like home as anywhere else could.

Somehow, the thought of *home* made her

remember the glimpse she had of Sebastian Barrett when they arrived in port. He was so different from the memory that had haunted her from London, so serious. What was he thinking about? Mary frowned—surely he was the last thing she should think of when she felt that old pang of longing for a place to belong.

A church bell tolled from outside the window, deep and sonorous, pulling her away from the unwelcome thoughts that haunted her about Sebastian. She glanced outside to the street below.

Most of the lanes they had bumped over in their night journey had been hard-packed earth, but the narrow road outside their house was made of cobbles. Shadows were cast over the moss-covered rocks, outlines of the tall, close-packed whitewashed houses, the balconies that jutted out from the upper stories, shaded in latticework.

It was still early and there weren't many people out and about yet, unless they were all clustered at the docks, waiting to catch a glimpse of the royal ships. Mary glimpsed women in sleeveless, pale muslin dresses against the warmth of the sun, mantillas draped over their heads and shoulders, the flash of diamonds around their necks and around their wrists. She had heard the large, shimmering stones were still mined in the interior of the country and worn by all the fine ladies all day long, and she wondered if her pearls would look paltry in comparison.

Intrigued, she leaned over the windowsill, craning her neck to try to glimpse the city's main square around the corner of their little lane. She knew from their passage last night that it was also cobbled, with the large, carved façade of the grand cathedral at one side, where the magnificent painted and bejewelled statue of the Madonna looked down on the marble front steps where the royal family would go to hear mass as soon as they disembarked. The lanes, cobbled and dirt alike, were swept clean and lined with fragrant flower petals and cinnamon sticks, already trampled underfoot and spreading their intoxicating fragrance on the breeze.

At the other side of the square was the new royal palace, a structure that had been quickly converted from the viceroy's small, rambling house. Mary had caught a glimpse of it in the moonlight, workmen still scrambling over it on ladders, converting it into walkways between an old prison with barred windows and the convent connected to the cathedral into a larger palace. Along with the smell of flowers and the faint whiff of salty sea air, she could smell fresh paint, the gilt that was being laid over the window frames. She thought of how, at least for a time, Dom Joao and Doña Carlota would have to live together again. She remembered Teresa mentioning how much the Princess hated her husband, the man she had been tied to since she was ten, how much she had tried to create her own powerful entourage in Europe. Now, here in Brazil, that was ended.

People were gathering outside now, atop the roofs and in windows, waiting for more of the fascinating spectacle of royalty to come into their midst.

'Mary, dear, are you ready? They shall be disembarking at any moment,' her father said as he hurried into the sitting room, looking most distracted, as he had far too often of late. He wore the full splendour of his courtly diplomatic dress, satin breeches and stocking, a dark-blue satin coat embroidered with gold braid and with his medals and ribbons. He looked just as handsome as she always remembered, but she worried at the dark circles beneath his eyes.

'Of course, Papa. But I fear I shall be quite overshadowed by your splendour!' she answered, forcing a cheerful smile to her lips as she rushed to his side. She straightened one of his diamond-framed medals. 'I see I shall have to beg for presents of more flashing jewels while we're here.'

'You can have anything you like, my dear, as you well know! But you look lovely, as always,' he said. He gently touched her cheek, a wistful smile on his face. 'Just like your mother.'

'No one could be as beautiful as Mama.' Mary linked her arm through her father's. 'Papa, is everything quite well? I mean—I know it is not. Thousands of people have just been hurled across the sea and you must help them come right again. But are *you* well? If we could find a good English doctor…'

'I am quite well, my dear, quite well,' her father insisted. 'The warm sun will do me good, I'm sure. Now, shall we go? We must be waiting for the royal arrival.'

Mary nodded. She knew he would not tell her more, not yet, not when he had a job to do. She would just have to make sure he rested, ate his meals and enjoyed something of this strange land they had found themselves in, just as she had to.

She caught a glimpse of herself in one of the mirrors just before they left the house. She was right, she thought, that her father's attire was much more splendid than hers! She wore a white gown, simply embroidered with tiny blue flowers and trimmed at the low, round neck with a fine lace frill, and her mother's white-lace mantilla covered her dark hair. Her face looked pale beneath its cobweb-delicate pattern, but she knew she looked as well as she could.

She wondered if Sebastian would think so, as well, and pushed that thought away. It should not matter to her in the least what he thought about her now!

In the crowded square, her father had to leave her to find his delegation, and he deposited her with a group of other ladies near the marble steps to the cathedral, out of the hot tropical sun. She studied the people around her, the press of the people who had long been living in Brazil in their pale cottons and fine gems and the stunned courtiers who had recently disembarked, stifling in velvets and gold embroidery. The air smelled of cinnamon and flowers, sweet on the warm breeze, along with the less lovely dirt of the streets, the press of people and horses in close quarters.

Mary glimpsed Sebastian across the square, the gleam of the sun on his golden-brown hair. He was taller than most of the men around him and his handsome face looked solemn and watchful above his fine white cravat. For an instant, Mary's breath caught at the sight of him and she quickly looked away. She could not be distracted by him, not now.

The doors to the cathedral opened and the crowd let out a loud cheer and surged for-

ward, carrying Mary with them. Sebastian
was quickly lost to her sight in the crush and
she couldn't even see her father any more. The
heat was even more intense there, the sunlight
brighter, the smells of the cinnamon and flowers and perfumes powerful, along with the in-
cense that flowed on a silvery cloud out of
the cathedral doors. Musicians launched into
a lively dance tune, blending with the church
bells and the cheers.

She managed to push her way to the edge of
the square, near the fountain and away from
the thickest of the press of people at the cathedral stairs. She went up on tiptoe to catch
a glimpse of the royal family as they emerged
from Mass.

They stopped beneath the vivid triumphal
arch to wave and Mary could hear a ripple of
disappointed murmurs around her. Unlike the
fabulous, idealised colour of the paintings, the
real figures were rather prosaic.

Dom Joao was short and portly. Even in
his vivid scarlet-satin coat, flashing with gold
braid and an array of jewels, he could not disguise his heavy frame and square, plain face,

his balding head and rounded shoulders. Yet he seemed rather pleased to be there, after all the long months of prevarication back in Lisbon about whether to stay or go. He bowed and smiled, waving the plumed hat in his hand at the crowd.

His wife, Doña Carlota, however, could not disguise her dismay. Mary remembered the tales of how grief-stricken the Princess was to leave Europe, the panicked letters she had sent to her Spanish family begging them to save her. The life she had made for herself, of her own palaces, her own lovers, her own power, she had to leave behind. Mary wondered how she must be feeling now, after all that struggle was in vain and now she found herself in a strange land across the ocean, with a husband she could not bear.

Doña Carlota seemed to stare at something far off, away from the curious and celebrating crowds. She held her head high, her expression stony and unreadable as she gazed over everyone's heads. Even shorter than her husband, and stout after so many children, she still managed to look more regal than him, in her plain black-velvet gown and flashing diamond jewellery. To cover her head, shorn after the plague of lice on her ship, she wore an elaborate silk turban pinned with a ruby star.

Around them were their children, the boys dressed in blue coats and knee breeches, the heir with a jewel-sewn coat like his father's and the girls in white gowns with black sashes. They all blinked out at the vivid crowds arrayed in the brilliant sunshine, as if shy and uncertain.

A small figure, swathed in black taffeta, was borne out on a chair litter. Mad Queen Maria, who was waving happily at the people, seemingly revived by the long voyage and her new home at the convent behind the cathedral.

Behind them came their attendants, gentlemen in their court clothes of satin coats and knee breeches, looking damp and misplaced in the bright tropical sun, and the ladies in their fine French fashions. Metallic embroidery on pale silks, long gloves, the ones who had escaped the lice with elaborate, upswept curls.

Mary caught a glimpse of Teresa behind Doña Carlota's diminutive figure and tried to wave at her. Teresa seemed to be searching the crowds, as if looking for something, a small frown on her face beneath the fluttering lace of her mantilla.

'Look at their gowns,' a woman behind Mary said with a giggle. 'Do you think that is how everyone dresses in Europe?'

'It's very pretty,' another lady said with a sniff. 'But surely they will suffocate in such things here! Not to mention no one will be able to afford finery like that. The shopkeeper Mr Daniels charged me five times what he should have, just for these ribbons!'

Dom Joao opened a heavy purse and tossed out a handful of coins in a shimmering silver archway into the crowd. A great cry exploded and everyone shoved forward again. The two women pushed against Mary and she was so startled she stumbled on the slippery cobblestones. She felt herself falling, the cold jolt of the fear, and her arms shot out to catch herself.

The hard blow of the cobbles never came. A strong arm locked around her waist, lifting her up higher to safety.

Mary knew who it was, even before she

twisted around in his arms to look down at him. She knew Sebastian's touch all too well now, the warm, hard security of it, knew the clean, citrus soap smell of him. He had rescued her too many times before.

He looked up at her with his jewel-green eyes and for an instant it seemed there was only the two of them in that crowded square.

'I do always seem to be in need of rescue when you're around, Lord Sebastian,' she said. 'It is most distressing.'

His handsome face, so solemn and concerned before, broke into a smile. That smile made his face even more beautiful, breathtakingly so. 'I'm just glad to be of service to you, Miss Manning. You usually seem to have little use for me.'

'Can you blame me?' she blurted, then immediately wished she could draw the words back. She never wanted him to know how much he had the power to hurt her. Not after how she felt when she learned the truth about her romantic dream in London.

Yet as she looked into his face now, she saw few echoes of that young man she thought she once knew. There were new lines on his face, hardening the good looks, a new solemnity in his eyes.

And she was no longer that girl, either, the girl who had once thought it was freeing to abandon caution and run heedlessly into her new, heady emotions. There were so many more important, more dangerous things in the world for them to worry about now.

She looked away, feeling her cheeks turn embarrassingly warm. She hoped it could only be blamed on the hot day, not on the fact that he was so near her again. After he changed ships on their voyage from Lisbon, she had thought she'd escaped him, that the weeks at sea would make her forget him. That once they met again, he would be much like any of the other handsome men she had met in her travels—charming, interesting for a moment, easily forgotten.

She realised now that had been foolish. Sebastian Barrett was *not* like any other men she had met. He never had been and never would be.

And that was why she had to be more careful around him. She couldn't let the intoxicating light of that place blind her.

After a long, tense moment of silence, Sebastian gave a grim nod. He slowly lowered her to her feet. 'I'm afraid I deserve that. But I assure you, Miss Manning, you have nothing to fear from me now.'

'Nothing?' Mary almost laughed. Surely she had more to fear of him than she ever had of anything else. With him, she had to fear herself, her own wild feelings, as she never had to before. Not only did she have the memory of how she had once kissed him, how he had once turned her away, but also she had to be careful of his real intentions there in Brazil. She had long ago learned that every person in a diplomatic delegation, especially men who were sent in the midst of delicate negotiations, often had their own, secret plans.

'I know you will not believe me, but I only want to keep you safe,' he said.

To her shock, Mary found that she *wanted* to believe him. 'Do you think I haven't learned how to keep myself safe, Lord Sebastian? That my family and friends cannot help me?'

'Miss Manning—Mary,' he said, in a quiet, strangely urgent tone that captured her attention fully. 'There are things happening here in Brazil—things you cannot know. You must be wary.'

'What do you mean?' she said, startled.

The crowd surged around them again, pushing her close against him. His arm came around her to hold her steady. 'Come with me,' he said close to her ear. His hand slid tight around hers and he pulled her with him against the wave of the crowd towards the edge of the square. His tall, lean body sheltered her from the cheering mass of people.

She went with him, unable to resist, to run away. She was far too curious to know what his words meant. Brazil was such a strange place, so full of light and heat, that she hadn't felt like herself ever since she glimpsed its shore. Being close to Sebastian now only made her feel even more the strange, heady glow of it all. Made her feel like a different person entirely.

He drew her into the shelter of a narrow walkway that ran between two of the white-washed buildings. The overhanging balconies blocked out the bright sunlight, casting strange shadows on the cobblestones below. The sound of the crowds, mere steps away, seemed muted and echoing there.

Mary looked up into Sebastian's face, searching his expression for some hint of what was happening. The shadows flickered over his sculpted face, casting his eyes into darkness.

She thought of her own strange feelings there in Rio, her father's distraction. Could something dangerous, even more dangerous than what was left behind in Lisbon, be happening? She reached out and gently touched his arm, half-afraid the feel of him would give her a lightning shock. But his hard, muscled strength seemed to give her something to hold on to for a moment in that shifting, tilting world.

'Please, Sebastian,' she said softly, not looking away from him. She saw something glimmer in his eyes at the sound of his name. 'What is happening? Is there something dangerous happening here in Rio? Something that could affect my father?'

Sebastian reached up and covered her hand

with his, his skin warm against hers. 'Mary, I fear I cannot talk about my work. But you surely know how much is at stake here. Just because the Braganzas are out of the paths of Napoleon and under British protection for now, it doesn't mean everyone is content with matters as they are. Everyone has their own ideas of the world as it should be.'

Mary's mind raced, whirling around all the dangers that lurked behind them in Europe. 'Do you mean the Prince Regent's position? If he really preferred the French alliance and he was forced to leave...'

'Perhaps not Dom Joao. He did seem to come around truly to the importance of the English alliance. But there are others, many others, who may still prefer France.' To her shock, he took both her hands in his and held them close. 'Mary, you have lived this life of diplomacy for a long time. I know you realise that things are seldom as they appear. But I also know that your kind heart thinks ill of no one—except dastards like me who deserve it.'

A dastard? It was true she had once thought that, but now she was not so sure. Mary's head was spinning. 'Who should I think ill of? My father confides little in me of his work; I know he doesn't want to worry me. But I do hear whispers, see things…'

'And you want to protect your family, as I do. I have come to see the real importance of family, Mary, whether you believe me now or not. I want to help you, if I can.'

'Please, Sebastian!' she cried. 'Tell me what is happening.'

He glanced over her shoulder, to the doorway where their quiet little sanctuary spilled out to the noisy square, and his expression hardened. As she watched, it went in an instant from urgent to cold as ice. Even though he still stood close to her, holding on to her hands, he seemed to have flown away from her.

She tried to tug her hands away, but he held on to her. He looked down at her again, his eyes dark.

'You are friends with the Fernandes siblings, yes?' he said, his voice quiet, chilly. 'Dom Luis and his sister?'

Mary was confused. 'Teresa? Yes, we became friends when I arrived in Lisbon and spent much time together on the voyage. She is lady-in-waiting to Doña Carlota...' Doña Carlota—who was famously discontented with the voyage to Brazil, with losing her Iberian power base. 'Are you saying that Teresa is helping Doña Carlota in her communications with her family in Spain, or something of that nature? I am sure that can't be true. Teresa thinks of little but fun, but she and her brother are loyal to their Queen and Regent.'

But was that really true? Mary remembered how Sebastian said her 'kind heart' wouldn't suspect a friend and she bit her lip. She did not want him to think her naïve, but neither could she imagine Teresa was a conspirator. Perhaps Sebastian was the one with darker motives, trying to plant doubts in her mind? How well did she know him, really?

'I fear I have no time to talk now, Mary,' he said quickly. 'And I know you do not, cannot, trust me again. Just please—be careful of all that happens around you.'

'I always do that. Sebastian, please, tell me what you mean!'

He raised one of her hands to his lips and

pressed a quick kiss to her wrist. His lips were warm through the thin silk of her glove. 'Will you be at the royal court? There is to be an official reception at the palace in two days.'

'Of course. Should I beware of something there? Really, Sebastian—I feel I am in a Gothic play of some sort.' And of course, she was. She had come with an entire royal court across an ocean to escape invasion and war; she was in the middle of hundreds of people, all with their own desires and agendas. It could be nothing but Byzantine.

He gave her a reluctant-looking smile. 'It is not, I promise. All too mundane in these times, I fear. I will find you at the reception and will tell you more if I can. Just promise me you will be careful.'

Mary stared up into his eyes. His hand on hers felt warm, safe, and she found that in that moment she did something she thought she never would—she trusted him. 'I will be careful.'

'Then let me help you find your father now.'

She nodded, knowing they could not stay there hidden much longer, that she couldn't yet force him to tell her what was in his mind. She followed him to the end of their walkway and they were plunged back into the chaos of the square. The royal family was processing from the cathedral to their makeshift palace, amid a shower of flower petals.

With every step, she was intensely aware of Sebastian pressed close to her in the crowd, his tall body sheltering her, his warning words ringing in her mind.

She would go along now. What choice did she have? She could not force him to tell her; indeed she was sure he was a man who could not be *made* to do anything. But she no longer would leave herself vulnerable, either.

'Mary! Mary, over here,' she heard Teresa call over the music and the cheers.

Mary glanced over her shoulder to find Teresa hurrying towards her, with Luis close behind her, both of them blindingly beautiful in their fine court clothes. Her white-lace mantilla fluttered in the breeze, studded with tiny, flashing crystal beads. Mary waved back to them.

When she turned back to Sebastian, she

found he was gone, melted away into the crowd as if he had never been there with her at all.

Teresa grabbed Mary's hand and drew her into the merriment of the square. The royal family had vanished into the palace, but the party still swirled on. Mary glimpsed her father talking to some of his colleagues on the cathedral steps, then he was gone as well, but not before she glimpsed the frown on his face.

'Mary, it is the most wonderful thing! There is to be a masked ball tomorrow night, here in this very square,' Teresa cried. 'Doesn't that sound like marvellous fun? We have to find a dressmaker immediately, to make up glorious gowns before anyone else can hire them.'

Mary laughed at her friend's enthusiasm, despite Sebastian's labyrinthine warnings about the Fernandes siblings. Surely he had to be wrong. Teresa was always so full of laughter, lightness, despite the loss of her home city. 'A marvellous gown in only a day?'

'I am sure it can be done. Come, we must start right away,' Teresa said, tugging Mary away down one of the crowded streets.

'And perhaps you would save me a dance,

Senhorita Manning?' Luis said, smiling down at Mary. He was certainly very handsome, almost as handsome as Sebastian in his dark, alluring way, and she tried to read his dark eyes, to see if he hid any secrets there. But there was nothing but laughter. 'A *carricola*? I could teach you.'

Before Mary could answer, Teresa rushed forward, drawing them both behind her. Mary laughed, letting herself be lost in the heady swirl of the moment, yet she did not forget her resolve to find out exactly what secrets Sebastian held.

Chapter Thirteen

Mary surveyed the drawing room, set up with tea for Teresa's visit with the dressmaker they had somehow bribed to make their costumes for that night's masked ball. All seemed to be in readiness, as elegant as she could make it in such a short time. The room was small, but pretty, with her mother's finely embroidered tablecloths and silver ornaments on every surface. The china tea service was laid out, along with an array of delicacies she had managed to communicate with the cook on making. Large arrangements of tropical flowers, bright pink and red and yellow, splashed their vivid colours over the pale walls.

From beyond the louvred doors of the dining room, which her father had set up as his makeshift library, she could hear him rustling papers and moving books about. He had been quiet over breakfast, smiling as she told him about the arrangements for the masked ball, but also distracted. She hoped she would not be in his way.

She moved a vase of flowers from one table to another, wondering why she felt so restless. Was it the sun, so golden-hot behind the shutters? The strangeness of the new place? The ball? She couldn't fathom it at all.

She just hoped it was not because of Sebastian. Surely that was not it!

Her whirling thoughts were interrupted when Teresa arrived, amid flurries of bonnet ribbons and feathers, exclamations of the loveliness of the room, the excitement of the ball. She was soon followed by the dressmaker and there was very serious work to commence.

Before long, the sitting room was scattered with lengths of bright silks and velvets, sheer muslins, spools of ribbon and lace, as fine as any that could have been found in Europe. Mary sipped at her tea and watched as the dressmaker finished with the hem of Teresa's costume, a frothy confection of white cotton and lace with delicate, silvery angel's wings.

The warmth of the sun flowing from the windows, the shadows that lurked in the corners, gave it all such a wondrous dreamlike feeling. She almost felt as if she was dreaming, watching the scene through a lacy veil. She remembered what her father had said about Sebastian and wondered if he would be at the masquerade. Would he tell her then what he had warned her about? Or would he evade her again?

He was so very maddening.

'What do you think, Mary?' Teresa asked, pulling Mary away from her thoughts of Sebastian. Teresa spun around, her sheer sleeves fluttering in the sunlight. 'Does it need more ribbons? More lace here?'

'I am afraid those are all the ribbons I have, *senhorita*,' the dressmaker said with a fierce scowl. 'Since the royal family has arrived, every scrap of silk and lace has been sold five times over! No one wanted such things before; almost no merchants would import them. Now they are all anyone asks for! How am I to run my business?'

'It doesn't need anything at all, Teresa,' Mary assured her. 'You will surely be the prettiest, most stylish lady at the party.'

Teresa laughed. 'I don't think there is much competition! Doña Carlota and her ladies, with their enormous turbans…' She snatched up a length of bright red-and-white-striped satin and wove it around her head in a towering arc. 'Dashing, yes?'

Mary had to laugh at the incongruous sight of the elaborate swath of fabric against the plain white walls, the warm sunshine. 'Very dashing indeed.'

'And what will you wear, Mary?' Teresa asked.

'I hardly know,' Mary said. 'Whatever is left, I suppose.'

'Ah, no, *senhorita*!' the dressmaker cried. 'I have brought one of my finest creations for you to try on. Something to go with your friend's angel gown.' She snapped her fingers and her assistant hurried forward with a muslin-wrapped parcel over her arms. They drew it back to reveal a gown and Mary gasped, for it was not what she would have expected.

It was made of glossy black satin, as lustrous as a starry night, with a simple skirt draped from a high waist which was bound with red ribbons. Black lace, delicate as cobwebs, fell from the square neckline. It made her think of the evenings aboard the ship during the voyage, the many shades of black in the sky that stretched endlessly over the ship; it was a gown for a queen of the night.

'Oh, Mary!' Teresa cried, hurrying over to carefully touch one of the black-lace ruffles. 'It's amazing.'

'Indeed it is,' Mary said, sitting up straight in her chair. 'But is it too—bold?'

'Not at all, *senhorita*!' the dressmaker protested. 'It will suit you most well. Shall you try it on now? There is much to be done if it's to be ready for tonight.'

'Yes, do, Mary,' Teresa urged. 'It will look beautiful. Every man there will want to dance with you, especially my brother.'

Mary laughed. Suddenly, she *did* feel bold. Luis Fernandes was very well known at the royal court as a flirt and great lover of ladies. She could not take him seriously, though he had asked her to dance; perhaps others would as well? And perhaps she *would* dance, safe behind her mask.

Safe from Sebastian.

She quickly slipped behind a screen set up in the corner of the room and quickly slipped out of her simple muslin morning dress into the basted-together gown the assistant handed her.

She caught a glimpse of herself in a gilt-framed mirror on the wall and was startled. She'd been so careful for so long, so respectable and proper. Ever since she had let her emotions take hold of her so foolishly in London, she had held herself in so closely. Now—now she wanted to fly, just a little bit. Was it this place? The sun and heat, the brilliant flowers and strange people?

Or was it—could it be—Sebastian again? His handsome face, his mysterious words. The way he looked at her, as if he saw her as no one else ever had.

She stepped out from behind the screen and the dressmaker rushed over with her pins and thread, clucking over the long, sheer sleeves, the unfinished hem. 'What do you think, *senhorita*?'

'It is beautiful, of course,' Mary said. 'Your skills would not be out of place in London or Lisbon, I'm sure.'

The dressmaker smiled smugly. 'I was told this style would suit you above all others, *senhorita*.'

Mary was startled. 'Told by who? My father?'

The dressmaker shook her head. 'Oh, no. Senhor Manning did indeed send for me, but a younger gentleman visited my shop only this morning. He had seen this satin in my window and wanted me to save it for you especially. He was most—persuasive.'

The assistant giggled.

'Who was this man?' Mary demanded.

The dressmaker shrugged. 'He was young, and quite handsome. You must have a secret admirer.'

'Oh, Mary!' Teresa cried. 'Could it be Luis? I did not know he had such romance in him.'

Mary stared at herself in the mirror, wondering about this 'secret admirer', her curiosity dangerously stirred. In the black-and-red gown, the mysterious veil of lace and silk, she would surely melt into the tropical night itself, searching its shadows for this admirer. Nothing could hide from her then.

Not even Sebastian Barrett.

Chapter Fourteen

The square where the ball was to happen was the same as the one where the reception had been held, bound by the makeshift royal palace on one side and the cathedral on the other, but it was completely transformed as the sun sank below the sea on glorious streaks of gold and crimson and purple.

The shutters of the mansions were thrown wide to let out even more amber light and flickering torches lined the cobblestones. The white façades of the buildings were draped with white flowers, tied with fluttering streamers in white and green and gold, waiting to greet the guests as they appeared as if by magic from the alleyways and from inside the houses.

Mary paused at the foot of the marble steps

of the cathedral to take in the whole magical scene. The nearly full moon, almost a pure silver in the dusty purplish-blue sky, shimmered down on the cobbled courtyard that was already full of revellers. They spun and twirled faster and faster in time to the music of the royal orchestra, which played from one of the balconies overhead. The song was quick and lively, full of drums and castanets to bring Iberia a bit closer. On another balcony, hung with cloth-of-gold, the royal family looked down on the party, remote and quiet, Doña Carlota's turban shining white and red, just as Teresa's had.

Long, white-draped tables laden with pastel-iced cakes and golden ewers of wine were laid out on one side of the fountain. It looked like everyone who was not dancing was clustered there, laughing over the streams of wine, recovering from the long voyage and the shock of their new home.

The flickering light of the torches reflected in the sparkling waters of the fountain and in the beads and jewels of all the fabulous costumes. Surely everyone had dragged out all their best finery, hauled across the ocean in the ships' holds, or cajoled from the local dress-makers, as Mary's and Teresa's had been. The dancers wove in and out of the lights, fan-tastic wraiths in black masks, brilliant satin gowns and velvet jackets, arrayed as all sorts of things. Saints and devils, gods and goddesses in pale draperies, dragons, butterflies, even sea monsters in glittering blue and green.

Mary searched every masked face that swirled past her, wondering if one of them concealed Sebastian.

'Oh, Mary, it is so beautiful,' Teresa said with a happy sigh.

'Most beautiful indeed,' Mary agreed. And it was, like an enchanted night spell where anything could happen. Where behind every mask could be the man of her dreams—her 'secret admirer.' A man who could imagine this fabulous costume would suit her.

Teresa was swept into the swirling dance by a man in a Tudor velvet doublet, handsome but surely rather stifling in the tropical night. Mary glimpsed her father near the refreshment tables, with a cluster of his diplomatic friends as always, all of them watching the frantic air of merriment with solemn, watchful faces. Her father *had* made an attempt at a costume, with a white linen toga wrapped over his dark-green evening coat, but he wore no mask. She waved at him and he seemed startled for an instant before he remembered who she was in her black lacy mask. He waved back with a smile.

Mary laughed. Could she truly be so well concealed behind her new gown? It made her feel bold indeed, like a different person, just for a short moment.

She made her way towards the flower-draped dais at the side of the cathedral, keeping to the edges of the dancing, boisterous crowd. The music was enthralling, the drums beating louder and louder as the dancers spun faster and faster. The music seemed to carry the wave of gaiety into the very sky itself. Even those who had been most angry at being cast across the sea, away from their home to this strange place, seemed carried away by the magic of it all.

As Mary reached the edge of the steps, a harlequin in black-and-white satin squares reached out and tried to pull her into the dance. She laughed and shook her head until he whirled away, but she found she *did* want to dance. Usually, she managed to stay safely, watchfully, on the sidelines. Yet tonight, that wonderful music, the flickering torchlight, the fantastical costumes, even the mysterious darkness of the night itself, seemed to call out to her with all its enticing possibilities.

But she only really wanted to dance in *one* man's arms. To find that giddy freedom she had only known once before. One which she shouldn't want at all now, not when Sebastian was so cloaked in mystery.

Mary closed her eyes for a moment behind her mask, closing out the dreamlike whirl. Why was he really there in Brazil, always waiting there to remind her of her own mistake in London? When she had found out the truth of him so long ago, the truth about her own young, foolish self, it had taken her a long time to find her balance again.

Now he was here again, even more intriguing than before.

Mary looked up and found the statue of

the Madonna in a niche high above, watching the merriment with her beautiful blue-glass eyes. She seemed to smile, as if she knew the strangeness of everything that happened under her serene gaze. Mary wished she could see so clearly herself.

She hurried behind the church, away from the noise of the party, finding a quieter walkway that reminded her of the one where Sebastian led her to whisper his warnings. She could still hear the music and laughter, could see the reflection of the torchlight on the white walls, but here she could at least take a breath and think a little more clearly.

When she closed her eyes, she saw Sebastian's face in her mind. She was not the same person she had been when they first met, so young and a bit scared in a new world in London. Surely he was not the same, either, but *how* had he changed? Or was he only different in the way she now saw him?

She heard a small sound, a rustle in the shadows behind her, and she spun around to see a cloaked figure standing at the entry of her walkway. She pushed herself away from

the wall, thinking to flee, then he put his hood
back and the light gleamed on Sebastian's sun-
streaked hair. She fell back a step, watching
him warily.

'Does the Queen of the Night not dance at
her own ball?' he asked, a half-smile in his
voice.

Was he the one who had told the dressmaker
to bring her the black satin? 'I—I fear she has
a secret,' she said, trying to match the lightness of the evening. She feared she was not so
good at counterfeiting emotion. 'She is a terrible dancer.'

'And too busy to practise? She has all the
stars to arrange, the spirits of the night to dis-
patch on their dark errands…'

Mary laughed. That sense of a dream party
grew around her, like a hazy cloud that suddenly made her forget all her caution, just
for a moment. It was almost as if the tropical
warmth had made her into a whole new person for that one night.

He looked so mysterious, so enticing, his
dark cloak making him a shadow against the
torchlight. He seemed to beckon to her with-

out even moving, his eyes glowing that bright green, like the sea beyond their party. She stepped closer to him, one careful, whisper-like movement, then another. He *had* warned her, after all, though she couldn't seem to stay away from him.

Her heavy black skirt and the fine lace of the ruffles trailed around her, the only thing that seemed to hold her to the ground. At last, she drew close to him, so close she could feel the warmth of him. He held himself perfectly still, his tall body tense, never taking his bright gaze from her face.

She dared to reach out and let her finger-tips trail over his cheek. She wore no gloves with her costume and his cheek felt so warm, so smooth under her touch, just slightly rough-ened over his chiselled jaw. She almost felt as if the vital heat of him, that glowing light like the tropical sun itself, flew into her. Just like the land itself, he seemed to coax her back into life.

'Is this a dream?' she whispered.

'If it is, I hope we don't wake up yet,' he answered.

His arms came around her, drawing her so close to him that nothing could come between them. She went up on tiptoe, twining her arms around his neck to hold him with her—or to keep herself from flying away into the sky. He drew her even closer and his lips swooped down to meet hers in a hard, hungry kiss.

They fit so perfectly together now, as if they had been made for this one moment. Mary parted her lips to meet his kiss, feeling the tip of his tongue touch hers, sliding closer to taste her deeply, as if he was as hungry for her as she was for him. She remembered that long-ago, too-fleeting kiss, and it was only a shadow to what she felt now with him.

The kiss turned frantic, full of need, full of the desperate desire to forget the past and have only *now*. As if London hadn't happened, as if there had never been their foolish, youthful selves. As if they were all of now.

She wanted that so much, she didn't protest at all when she felt him press her back against the rough, whitewashed wall. His moan echoed against her lips and his hands were hard and hungry as they slid over her shoulders, over the curve of her breasts in the tight satin bodice. Mary sighed at the delicious friction, the new, wonderful sensations that shivered through her.

A loud crack burst over them and for an instant she feared it was her heart, opening to this mysterious, changeable man all over again. She pushed herself away from him and saw that it was fireworks arcing in a shimmering green-and-white arc over the rooftops. She tilted her head back, trying to breathe, but she couldn't do that with his touch on her. With him so very close.

He raised his head, suddenly tense and wary as a jungle cat. Mary turned away from him, tugging her new gown into place and drawing the long folds of her lacy veil to cover the heat of her cheeks. She had no doubt she was blushing bright red, all her confusion written on her face!

She drew in a deep breath, and then another, letting the smells of smoke and flowers clear her hazy mind. The mind that had only known *him* for those heady moments. Surely she could not have been so foolish again?

Yet she did not feel so foolish. She felt almost as if she could soar away into the sky.

'Mary,' he said hoarsely. 'I did not plan this, I promise. I am…'

'No,' she whispered, still not looking at him. Instead she watched the fireworks, red and gold in the black sky. 'Please don't say you're sorry. I could not bear it.' She couldn't bear it if he was sorry for this one perfect moment.

His hand slid down her arm, his fingers twining with hers for an instant. 'I fear I am not sorry at all. But I don't want to hurt you.'

'You can't,' she said. 'Tell me, Sebastian— were you the one who told the dressmaker to bring me this gown?'

He laughed, but did not answer. Then she knew he had, yet she still did not know why. Another part of his enigmatic warnings?

'Thank you,' she murmured. Yet she still didn't dare look at him, for fear she would not be able to walk away. She laughed, too, hoping it sounded light, careless, as if she did that sort of thing all the time—kissing in darkened walkways, moving through the night as if she was indeed its Queen. She hurried on her unsteady feet back to the crowded torchlight of the square, to the noise and movement of real life.

Sebastian braced his palms against the rough, whitewashed wall, his eyes closed as he forced himself to breathe deeply, slowly. To try to calm the fire that raged inside of him. He could still smell the sweet roses of Mary's perfume, as if she still lingered there with him. As if she was all around him, haunting him.

His hands curled into tight fists as he thought of her, her smile, the way she looked up into his eyes, as if she could see what he tried so hard to hide.

That raw longing for her, for her nearness, had to be conquered. It distracted him from his reason for being in Brazil. He had to keep the British alliance with the Portuguese Prince safe, at all costs.

The young, reckless man he had been when he met Mary in London, stunned by the grief of losing his friends in battle, would never have thought this way about duty. His duty to England, to his family—even to Mary, of the amends he owed her. That young man wouldn't have held back the surge or urgent desire that came over him when he tasted her lips.

But he was no longer that man. He had changed his life, his way of seeing the world around him. He had to prove that to himself and, more than that, he had to prove it to Mary.

Sebastian laughed ruefully at himself. Who would have imagined, if they saw him even a few years ago, that he would be so concerned about *honour*? With what anyone, even his family, thought of him? Mary, with her quiet, serious grey eyes, had changed him.

And now he had to prove that to her. He had to keep her safe, no matter what.

Chapter Fifteen

Teresa tiptoed along the makeshift-palace's terrace, careful to make sure she wasn't seen. It was very late at night, most of the revellers tucked up in their beds, the lamps extinguished. Doña Carlota was still awake, as she was late into most nights, but she would not need her ladies. She was writing furious letters to her Spanish family, raging against being torn away from Europe.

But she couldn't let anyone see her, even a footman. Teresa drew the hood of her cloak closer around her. High overhead, the moon shimmered in the dusty black sky, so unlike anything she had ever seen in Portugal. The scent of flowers hung heavy in the air, and she could hear the remnants of music from some-where far away.

She made her way to a quiet corner where her brother said she should wait for him and took a deep breath of the warm air. She only wanted to run back to her small room, to climb under her bedclothes, until this new life made some sense. Until she could find a way to flee again. But Luis would find her.

He would always find her, chasing her until she helped his schemes, just as he had since they were children.

For an instant, she thought of Mr Nicholas Warren, of his kind smile, the admiration in his eyes when he looked at her. She had many admirers; they had always seemed to be there, ever since she was a girl, but they never seemed to see *her*. They saw her family, or the beauty she had not created for herself. Never what was inside her heart, her longing to be free.

And Luis said it would always be thus, that he would be her only friend, her only family, and she had no reason to doubt that. Not until she met Mary Manning and had a real, female friend for the first time. Now she could see more, could imagine more. If only it were not too late!

'What have you discovered, Sister?' Luis said quietly, emerging from the shadows near the whitewashed wall.

Teresa shivered, hating the way he could move so quietly when he wanted to. 'Nothing yet. I told you, I can find out nothing of import for your friends at court. I only hear bits of gossip, the same as anyone.'

'But gossip is the one thing that will help us now!' He came to stand next to her at the stone railing, the tropical moonlight gilding his face, as handsome as hers was beautiful. It had always been their strength, even when their family fortune was mostly gone. 'We had no choice but to leave Lisbon now, but if we are to make our way home soon, we must be wise about it. We must not be drawn in by these English. They have their own goals and none of them involves the good of Portugal. They must help us now, even if they don't know it.'

Teresa nodded. She had heard those words so often, but she did not quite believe them.

She had heard the tales of what happened to countries when they were overrun by Napoleon's armies. But there was no denying they had been torn away from their homes, tossed on to this strange shore, and she wanted to go home again.

Even if that meant working with her brother.

'Miss Manning knows nothing,' she said. 'She keeps her father's house, but I don't think he confides in her. She doesn't care for politics.'

Luis laughed. 'I cannot believe that! We must stay with her, cultivate her friendship.'

Teresa nodded silently. Luis suddenly grabbed her arm, giving her a hard shake. She cried out and tried to pull away, but he held her fast. His eyes glittered like hard diamonds in the starlight.

'I mean what I say, Teresa,' he said. 'This is vital if we are to get home again. The English must help us—whether they like it or not. You *must* help me, it is your duty as a Fernandes. As a lady of Portugal.'

Her duty. She had heard that all her life. When did *she* get to choose? To be free to be kind, as Mary was kind? 'I will do my duty,' she said quietly. Her brother stared down at her, as if he could read her thoughts. She made her expression as bland as possible, her eyes cast down to the cobbles of the plaza below her.

Finally, he nodded and let her go. She backed away, rubbing at her arm. 'I must return to my bed now,' she said.

'Of course. The Princess cannot miss you. Just remember well what I said—the English are not your friends.'

Not her friends—she had been told that for so long. But, for the first time, Teresa could not quite believe it.

Chapter Sixteen

'Mary! You are very far away today. Have you been listening to me at all?'

Startled, Mary looked to Teresa where she sat on the seat across their small, open carriage. Teresa grinned at her and Mary had to laugh. In truth, she had *not* been listening ever since they left the city centre of Rio for an exploratory visit into the countryside. She couldn't stop thinking about Sebastian, about the wondrous unreality of their kiss, of the whole masked ball. She couldn't help but think it might all have been a dream. Now there was a picnic on the beach to get to and she had to cease dreaming.

And yet she was sure she could still fell his touch on her skin, still taste that kiss. She had been swept away by the whole romance of the night, the warm, flower-scented air, the freedom of a costume, the music. What had made him kiss her? Was it all a game again? What had he warned her about?

It had not felt like a game. But she had been mistaken about him before.

She tilted her parasol to shield the bright sun that burned over their open carriage. She knew she shouldn't worry about Sebastian Barrett and what he was really doing here in Brazil, here with her. Not at that moment. It was a beautiful day and she had never seen anything like the scene around them. The city itself had been crowded, noisy, bustling with a marketplace set up around the fountain in the main square, but here in the foothills it was quiet, flickering with shadows from the tall coconut trees. The city was spread out below them in a tumble of red roofs and white walls, with the surging sea beyond. The beach looked like a shimmering cream-coloured ribbon in the brilliant sun.

'I'm sorry, Teresa,' she said. 'I was just admiring the lovely scenery. It's so very different from anything else I've ever seen.'

Teresa nodded and also turned to study the mystery of the jungle that climbed above them into the black mountains. The wide brim of her pink-straw hat concealed her expression. 'It is hard to imagine it is winter at home right now. The sun is so blinding. It quite makes me forget…'

The note of melancholy in her usually cheerful friend's voice worried Mary. 'Are you quite well, Teresa?'

Teresa smiled. 'Very well indeed. Just a flash of homesickness, I think. But that will soon be gone. There are too many lovely distractions here. Are you going to the Countess de Graumont's party at her new beach villa tomorrow? It should be even more exotic than the masquerade.'

'We did receive an invitation this morning,' Mary said. She remembered the pile of cards already on their breakfast table, but her father had been most distracted when she asked him which parties they should attend. *Whatever you think best, my dear,* he had said before leaving her for his work. 'I am certainly looking forward to seeing the place. Will Dom Joao and Doña Carlota be there?'

Teresa laughed. 'Together, do you mean? I suppose they will; they are much thrown together now. I fear for what might happen if the Princess does not get her own home soon.'

Mary frowned, thinking of Sebastian's mysterious warnings that all was not well in Brazil, that she should be very careful. 'What do you mean? Is there some danger?'

'No more than usual, I think. It has been a long time since they lived together. Doña Carlota has become accustomed to having her own life, her own—base of power, shall we say. Luckily for me, I am only a very junior lady-in-waiting and only have to attend her on ceremonial occasions. Even then I have seen her Spanish temper explode when she has been too long near her husband.'

Mary nodded. Everyone knew how volatile the royal marriage was, how Doña Carlota had tried so hard to keep from coming to Brazil. That she had once before tried to overthrow her husband. Was it happening again?

Was that what Sebastian meant? 'Has anything happened of late? I have certainly heard the Princess would prefer to return to her Spanish family.'

'I am sure she would, but she cannot. Not now. Even if—' Teresa suddenly bit her lip and looked away. 'I think she does mean to find her own villa, some place near the water like the Countess de Graumont has done. I think I would enjoy a place like that, too.'

The carriage jolted around a turn in the road, giving them a sudden view of the ocean crashing below the rocky ledge of the hills. 'I would, as well.'

The ocean was indeed gloriously beautiful, but also most changeable instant by instant. It surged from palest turquoise blue to deep green, frothed with lacy white waves, crashing wildly over the sandy shore and receding back again. It made her think of Sebastian and how hard to read he was. How much he had changed since last she saw him, but how untrustworthy that was.

Suddenly, a flash of movement from the corner of her eye caught her attention. She turned her head to the mountains that rose above their path, to the dark cliffs that loomed above the jungle-like tree line. The hills were a dark purple-blue, shadowed, with small black openings dotted along the winding, paler paths.

Everything was very still now, just the wind in the trees the only movement, but she could have vowed she saw something up there, light and flashing against the darkness.

'What is up that way?' she said.

Teresa also glanced up, but she didn't seem terribly interested. 'Where, Mary? The hills?'

'They're the caves of the old people, *senhorita*,' their driver said.

Mary turned to look at him, perched above them on his box. He was a large man, dark-haired and square-faced in his new fine livery. The man who rented the Manning house to them, along with the staff, said the driver and his family were Portuguese who had lived in Brazil for some time, so hopefully he would know of the local places. 'The caves of the old people?'

He laughed. 'Not old like grandfathers, *senhorita*, but the civilisation that lived here before us, long ago. They lived up in those caves, but no one goes there now. It's too rocky and treacherous up the pathways. I have heard tell a few people who still worship the old gods make their way there once or twice a year, but I have never tried it. My wife scares our children away from them with tales of phantoms.'

'Fascinating.' Mary studied the looming hills, wondering at their mysteries. 'I thought I saw someone there just now.'

'I wouldn't go up there if I thought there were phantoms,' Teresa said with a laugh. 'I am sure it was just a shadow, Mary.'

'Yes, probably,' Mary murmured. But as they drove on, winding their way down to the beautiful beach, she glanced back at the mountains and shivered a bit. Their dark mystery was alluring, even as she knew she should stay far away. Just as it was with Sebastian.

As the carriage slowly lurched along the winding, narrow pathway towards the beach, even Teresa grew quieter, watching the passing scenery, the rocky road and the thick greenery with an expression of some concern. But Mary was glad of the silence for a moment, broken only by the creak of the carriage wheels, the cry of the birds in the thick, dark canopy of trees. She had to help her father, to keep watch over the social scene of their new home, and she couldn't be distracted so much by Sebastian Barrett.

But her worries vanished as the carriage suddenly emerged from the shadowed thicket and the sweep of the beach came into view. Bright white picnic pavilions were set up on the pale sand, colourful banners fluttering from every corner, and beyond was the rush of the aquamarine-and-emerald sea. In the distance she could glimpse the peaks of the distant mountains, purplish-black against the brilliant blue sky.

'Oh, how lovely!' Teresa cried. 'We shall have such fun today, won't we, Mary?'

Mary smiled. 'It is quite pretty. Like a medieval tournament in a story. If there had been sandy beaches then, of course!'

'So different from Lisbon,' Teresa said softly, as if to herself as she studied the glorious sweep of white and blue. 'It could be a lovely new beginning. If only Luis could see that…'

Mary frowned at her friend's sad tone. 'Does your brother not feel—settled here as of yet?'

Teresa laughed. 'Of course not. But surely he will see everything different in such a place as this.'

The carriage lumbered to a halt next to the other vehicles left haphazardly at the edge of where the rocky, green underbrush met the drifts of pale sand. Mary followed Teresa as they made their way towards the party, where sounds of music and laughter drifted out from the pavilions.

Mary's half-boots sank a bit into the sand, slowing her down, but she had to laugh. The warm breeze, smelling of salty sea and strange, heady flowers, caught at her bonnet and raised her spirits. Teresa was surely right—life looked very different in such a place.

She peeked up at the sky from beneath the ribbon-trimmed brim of her bonnet, dazzled by the glittering sunlight.

'Mary, hurry up!' Teresa called.

Mary quickly followed her friend into the

waiting pavilion. For a moment, the shadow after the bright light dazzled her and only slowly could she make out the scene before her. Long tables, spread with white-damask clothes and platters of fruit and fine cheese, iced cakes and creams, led up to a velvet-draped dais where Prince Joao sat with some of his children, all of them dressed in heavy satins and watching the merry gathering as if they were at a theatre. It seemed the Princess had not attended, but no one appeared to miss her very much. A small orchestra played dance music as everyone feasted and laughed.

Yet none of the crowd caught her attention as much as the man who stood near the dais. Sebastian; of course he would be there. He smiled, though he seemed rather apart from the party in his plain dark-blue coat and cream-coloured waistcoat. After only an instant, he vanished among the crowded tables.

A footman offered Mary a glass of pale-pink punch and she took it, glad of the distraction. She took a sip and choked on an unexpected sharp, strong rush of alcohol.

'One should go slowly with this punch, Miss

Manning—the Prince has been insisting everyone try the local rum, with startling effect,' Sebastian said behind her.

Mary whirled around, surprised and yet also warmly pleased. 'Really, Lord Sebastian! You *must* cease startling me so.' But she also had to laugh. Perhaps it was the warm day, the punch—or Sebastian's bright-green eyes, his teasing smile. It made her feel so much lighter, as if she could float away into the bright blue sky.

'How much of it have *you* imbibed, Lord Sebastian?' she asked.

'Oh, only the merest sip, I assure you,' he said, very seriously, yet there was that twinkle in his eyes. It made her think of when they had first met in London and she had been immediately drawn to his charm, which ought to have made her most cautious indeed.

Yet somehow that hard edge that had once given him a steel tinge seemed gone today and so was her chilly caution. She wanted to laugh and dance, too. To think he was the man she had once imagined.

'Perhaps we should try just a bit more, then,' she whispered.

Sebastian laughed, his eyes widening as if he was surprised at her words, but he fetched her a fresh glass of punch and they strolled around the edge of the crowd. Mary carefully sipped at her punch and studied the people around her, Portuguese courtiers and English friends of her father, but she was always warmly aware of the man who walked beside her. When she peeked up at him, she found him smiling down at her, as if he, too, felt the exotic loveliness of the day. She gave him a tentative smile in return.

'Is your father not here today, Miss Manning?' he asked.

Mary shook her head. 'He said he wanted to work at our lodgings today and I confess I was glad when he decided not to journey out of the city. I fear he has been working too hard lately.'

Sebastian nodded thoughtfully. 'Sir William is the most diligent of the English party, certainly, and his wisdom and experience have been most helpful to me. I hope he is not feeling unwell?'

'He says not, that I fuss over him too much and he is probably right.' Mary laughed at herself. 'I am always pressing cups of tea and shawls on him, poor Father. But it has been only the two of us for so long.'

'Anyone can see how much you care about each other,' he said and Mary thought she heard a small note of sadness deep in his voice. But when she studied him closer, he smiled again, chasing away the quick shadow in his eyes. 'I will join you in keeping careful watch on him. Perhaps he would let me help him in his work sometimes.'

'I would much appreciate any help you could give him, Lord Sebastian. I do think the warm sun has done him much good.' They stopped near an open doorway in the pavilion and Mary found herself gazing out at the sea beyond. 'And who would not? It is so beautiful here, sometimes I think it is a dream.'

'This is indeed a dream,' he said quietly and she looked up to find he watched not the blue-green waves, but her own face. She felt her cheeks turn warm and looked away.

She wandered on to the sand, spread just

beyond the party with carpets, but stretching beyond in a warm, white-gold sweep towards the waves. 'I did read much about Brazil on the journey, but I could not have imagined this. When I was a little girl, my mother read me a fairy story set in a tower by the sea in France and I think I envisioned it rather like this. I was very disappointed when I finally saw it and found it grey and cold! My mother would have loved this.'

'Do you remember much of your mother?'

'Not as much as I wish I did, of course. She was beautiful and always full of laughter. She would sing to me and hold me in her arms as we danced across the nursery! I don't think she ever thought I would even see her home of Portugal, let alone Brazil. What was *your* mother like?'

'My mother?' he said and sounded surprised.

Mary laughed. 'Yes. Surely even the lovely Lord Sebastian Barrett had a mother!'

'Of course I did. Do,' he said ruefully. 'But I don't think she is much like your mother. She has always been very quiet. She mostly listens while my father talks. And talks.'

Mary thought of the little her father had told her about Sebastian's father, who had long worked in the same diplomatic circles as her own family. *A perceptive man in his work,* her father had once said. *A credit to his name. But perhaps not as perceptive as he could be in other ways?*

Not as perceptive as a parent? Mary felt a pang of sadness, but his brilliant smile wouldn't let her feel sorry for him.

'I think this sight would make even my father be quiet for a moment!' he said and Mary laughed as he ran into the frothing edge of the surf as it broke up on the sand. 'It's warmer than a bath.'

Mary laughed again, and as the light beamed down on her, warm and golden and pure, she felt her heart lift just a bit. 'You will ruin your fine shoes!'

'It's worth it! Come, Miss Manning, wade in just a bit closer.'

She tiptoed just a tiny bit nearer the water, the music of its rush in and out a glorious symphony that blended with his laughter. He caught her hand in his and twirled her around, just like those dances she remembered from her childhood. It was wonderfully giddy and she closed her eyes for a moment to let it all swirl around her.

When she opened her eyes, she looked up at him, laughing, and found he smiled down at her. For an instant, she longed to lean closer to him, to touch his lips with hers, the past burned away in the sunshine, and he stared down at her intently.

'Mary! What are you doing? Your gown will be ruined,' she heard Teresa call and it was like a tiny shard of ice in the heat of the sun.

She drew back from Sebastian and turned to see Teresa and Luis waiting for her in the doorway of the pavilion. Teresa was laughing, too, but Luis looked far more solemn than Mary had ever seen him. Why would he care if she was laughing with Sebastian, wandering too near the waves?

But they did remind her of where she was, *who* she was. And who Sebastian was.

She gave him a quick curtsy and hurried

back to the party. Yet she was sure she could still feel his hand on hers and smell the flowers on the salty sea breeze.

Chapter Seventeen

'Are you perchance going to the Countess de Graumont's reception today, Lord Sebastian?'

Sebastian turned in the palace doorway, surprised to hear Sir William Manning speak to him. Sir William was always pleasant when they met, always willing to impart advice, but he was also very polite, somewhat distant, as if his thoughts were always far away.

Sebastian could see now what Mary had worried about, for Sir William did look rather tired. It had been an exhausting journey, frustrating to try to corral Prince Joao's indecisiveness. But Sir William's smile was friendly, open—much like Mary's.

'I am indeed, Sir William,' he answered. He hurried back to Sir William's side so they

could make their way out of the palace together, the cool shadows of the whitewashed
building blending into the heat of the morning.
'I am sure we deserve some diversion after the
meetings today.'

Sir William laughed ruefully. 'The Prince
can be difficult to keep to the topic, can he not?
England got him here; now I suppose we must
keep him happy in his new kingdom.'

'I am not sure a party where his wife will
be present would accomplish that.'

Sir William grimaced. 'That is much too
true, I fear. But at the moment we have little
choice—he does insist on going to the countess's reception. Come, Lord Sebastian, will
you walk with me for a moment? I feel the
need to stretch my legs.'

'Of course, Sir William.'

They made their way into the plaza outside
the temporary royal palace. Local women in
their white blouses and bright skirts did their
washing in the fountain, while children chased
past, shrieking happily in the pretty morning
light. A group of nuns hurried past, like a flock

of ravens in the colour and light, as the bells of the cathedral rang out the hour.

As Sebastian looked around, he remembered the masked ball, the exotic blend of darkness and light in the night where he had held and kissed Mary.

'I must confess, I was not entirely sure of your fitness for a job like this, not at first,' Sir William said, quietly, affably, almost as if he talked to himself.

Sebastian looked at him in surprise and found Sir William smiling faintly at him. 'I suppose not. I have been with the Foreign Office for little time, compared to my father and my late brother.'

'And when last we were both in London, you were known as something of a rogue, I fear. An Army hero, to be sure, but rather rackety. Not someone I would want my daughter talking to very much, perhaps. Once I did have hopes she might marry your brother, but then I came to see they would not suit. Lord Henry was much too methodical and pragmatic for my daughter. But you are doing very well in your brother's profession, I must admit.'

Sebastian nodded, remembering how Henry and his father had praised Sir William's work in the past. He felt foolish for forgetting how long Sir William had been a diplomat; how much he must see without words. But he also wanted this man to know how he had changed. It seemed very important. 'It was a few years ago. I fear I had not yet found my way.'

Sir William watched him steadily, still with that small smile on his face. 'My father was also a diplomat and I confess that until I married my Maria and was given my first posting on my own, I had a hard time finding my own talent as well. I hope you feel you have now. You have performed most admirably on this strange journey of ours, Lord Sebastian. You have a cool head, a sense of rightness—those are important attributes in this work.'

'I do hope you are right,' Sebastian said, most gratified by Sir William's words. If he could earn this man's respect, maybe it was even possible to earn Mary's in the end. 'And perhaps, one day, I could be a man your daughter *would* wish to talk to?'

Sir William laughed. 'Mary has a stubborn

heart sometimes, just as her mother did. She has a sense of how things should be, a goodness, just as you do. I fear she worries about me too much and I worry my work has kept her from living the life any young lady deserves. We have moved from city to city so much she has not had much time for things like friends and dancing. She will have to be persuaded carefully to give her heart to the right person in the end.'

'Miss Manning would be a great prize for anyone,' Sebastian said carefully.

'Indeed she would. Well, Lord Sebastian, this is my lodgings. I am glad we had time for a small talk. I shall see you at the reception, yes?'

Sebastian glanced up at the house whose doorstep they had landed on, a tall, narrow whitewashed dwelling with a red-tiled roof and black shutters. He wondered if Mary watched from behind one of those windows.

'Of course, Sir William,' he answered. 'I look forward to it.'

'But maybe you look forward to seeing my daughter more, eh?' Sir William's laughter faded into the warm breeze as he made his way into the house.

Sebastian had to laugh, too. Yes, he much looked forward to seeing Mary again. And, what was more, he had sudden hope she looked forward to seeing him, as well.

The Countess de Graumont's villa near the beach had once belonged to a lieutenant of the colonial governor, Mary had heard, and he had given it up to one of Doña Carlota's favourite ladies-in-waiting. Mary could definitely see why the countess had coveted the place. It was not large, but it was exquisitely beautiful, shimmering white in the moonlight, with long terraces lined with open windows to let in the ocean breezes, lit up like a Chinese lantern in the night. Just beyond the curving drive and the length of pale sand, Mary could see the breaking white waves on one side and the rise of the dark hills on the other. In the darkness, she couldn't see the caves she and Teresa had driven past, but the hills seemed to watch their revels in ancient silence.

Her father helped her from their carriage at

the foot of the marble front steps and she took his arm as he led her into the house, past the rows of flickering torches and the footmen in the countess's velvet livery, despite the warmth of the night.

Inside the ballroom, everything was as sparkling as it would have been at a courtly night in Lisbon. The men in their dark evening clothes and the ladies in their satin gowns swirled around to the strains of an orchestra, while the royal couple looked on from a gallery above. It seemed everyone was most determined nothing would change, despite the strangeness of their new home.

'I must meet with Mr Warren and some of his friends, my dear,' her father said, his face distant and distracted, just as it had been ever since they arrived in Brazil. 'Will you be all right on your own for a time?'

'Of course, Papa,' Mary answered. 'I will find Teresa and have a good gossip. But are you sure you are quite all right? Should you not eat something before you work? You had hardly anything at dinner.'

He gave her a smile, but she could see the

strain underneath. 'I am very well, Mary, I promise. I won't be long.' He quickly kissed her cheek and disappeared into the crowd.

Mary flicked open her lace fan and studied the gathering around her. She glimpsed Teresa in the gallery with the Princess and waved at her. Teresa pulled an agonised face, which was quickly concealed behind a smile as Doña Carlota turned to her. Mary laughed and made her way towards the refreshment tables laid out near the windows of the terrace.

Would Sebastian be there that night? She had wondered that too many times since their kiss at the masked ball. She went up on tiptoe and glimpsed him on the dance floor, his blonde waltz partner laughing up at him. He smiled down at her and they were swallowed up in the swirling figures of the dance.

Mary turned away, reaching for a glass of wine from a passing footman's tray. It should not matter at all to her whom he danced with; it did *not* matter. Yet she could feel the warmth in her cheeks.

Teresa and a group of other chattering, laughing ladies-in-waiting were in the cor-

ner and Mary hurried over to join them. In
their stream of gossip, she could almost forget about Sebastian—until she turned and saw
him walking towards her across the room.

She swallowed hard and just tried to keep
smiling, all too conscious of the other ladies
watching him.

'Miss Manning,' he said with a bow. 'Would
you do me the honour of dancing with me?'

Dancing? Mary smiled back, but she feared
she could not remember any dance steps at all.
Not when he was looking at her. But years of
being dignified in foreign courts stood her in
good stead now and she managed not to col-
lapse into girlish giggles.

'I thought I would not dance this evening,
Lord Sebastian,' she answered. 'But perhaps
a turn about the room?'

He nodded and offered her his arm. They
moved away from the other ladies and Mary
could feel them watching. 'I think—I may
need a breath of fresh of air,' she whispered.

'I quite agree with you,' he said with a
laugh. 'Perhaps a small glimpse of the beach?
It is quite beautiful in the moonlight.'

Mary nodded and slipped with him out of the half-open doors to the night beyond.

The sea under the moonlight was quite magical. Mary was captured by the sight of it, unlike anything she had seen before coming to Brazil. And Sebastian by her side made it all even more dreamlike.

She glanced up at him, at the elegant angles of his face limned by the moonlight. She thought of the rather vivacious lady who had been hanging on to his arm when she first saw him in the ballroom. Perhaps she herself did not have a flirtatious laugh or large, batting eyes, but surely she and Sebastian did share one very important thing—a concern for the British mission in Brazil. Surely they could speak the same language if they tried?

And then there had been that kiss at the masked ball…

Mary drew in a deep breath and turned away to look at the water again. She didn't dare let him know that she thought far too often about that kiss and the way it had swept her away like those very waves.

'Are you quite well this evening, Miss Manning?' he asked, his voice so deep and warm it seemed to touch her physically, brushing over her skin like the warm ocean breeze. 'I fear the royal contingent has been keeping rather late nights.'

She almost laughed at his careful words. 'Are you asking if I am rested after the midnight masked ball?' she said. 'Indeed. A good night's sleep and a strong pot of tea can do wonders, I have found.'

He laughed ruefully. '*Did* you sleep well, then?'

'Hardly at all, I confess. I had such dreams...'

'Dreams of masked figures in the darkness?'

Dreams of *him*, of course, but she would not say that aloud. 'I hardly remember. I do wonder why the Portuguese don't make every ball a masked ball. It would give them so much to gossip about. Royal courts do seem to enjoy gossip above all else.' She thought of what Teresa had whispered about on their carriage ride, secrets that every courtier held in such a divided royal family. 'Perhaps that is all they have to occupy them here, so far anyway.'

'But not us, of course,' Sebastian said teasingly. 'We English are above gossip.'

Mary laughed. Of course they were not above gossip—that seemed to be the best way she had always had of helping her father, listening to what ladies said in drawing rooms. But the chatter here confused her more than anything.

Sebastian held out his arm again, and she slipped her gloved hand into the crook of his elbow. His arm felt so strong, so warm under her touch. He led her in a slow stroll along the beach, past a few other couples who had ventured out into the flower-scented night.

'Perhaps I do indulge in a bit of frivolous conversation now and then,' she said.

'You? Miss Mary Manning? Never!'

'Sadly true,' Mary said with a sigh. 'So often there is not much else for us ladies to do at diplomatic postings.'

'And what do you whisper about?'

Men like you, of course, she almost said. 'Oh, many things. Fashion, of course. Hats, fans and shoes. Aren't all ladies interested in that, no matter where they are?'

Sebastian shook his head. She could feel him watching her, his eyes very serious, as if they could see too much. She kept her own gaze on the ocean. 'Some ladies, perhaps. But not you. You cannot fool me, Miss Manning.'

She hoped she *could* fool him, at least some of the time. Or all her years of diplomatic training had been wasted.

And he really couldn't be allowed to know that she was—horrors!—beginning to like him again.

There. She had admitted it, at least to herself. She looked forward far too much to moments like this, when she saw him again, when she could talk to him, feel his touch.

'Well, we do sometimes talk about hats,' she said. 'But sometimes of other things. Surely you have learned by now that, in the diplomatic world, the most interesting things can be learned in the most seemingly innocuous conversations?'

He was silent for a long moment. 'I have learned something of that, yes.'

Mary studied his face in the moonlight. How he had haunted her after London, with his handsome features, his reckless smile. Now here he was, the same, but not the same at all. He looked older in the night, more solemn. Even more intriguing.

'What did bring you into this diplomatic career, Lord Sebastian?' she asked quietly. 'You seemed to do very well in the military life.'

He gave her a wry little smile. 'I found I could save more lives in this work than I could as a soldier.'

Mary was surprised by his words, by his dark tone. 'But you were a hero.'

Sebastian shook his head. 'I did—I could do—no more on the battlefield than any other man in the regiment. I watched good men, men far better than I could ever be, die in horrible ways and I could do nothing to prevent it. I saw what my father had done in his career, what my brother Henry was set to do.'

'And that was?'

'To try and prevent battles before they even happened, with the force of their words. Our family has long made a name for themselves in diplomacy, but I fear it took the most horrifying of circumstances for me to see the real value of that.' He gave a wry laugh. 'Of course, it pained me to give my father the satisfaction of seeing me follow the family calling after so many years of kicking over the traces, but so it had to be. I have become respectable, Miss Manning.'

Mary laughed, remembering the young man she had met in London. The young man who had broken her heart. 'And how is your reform working, Lord Sebastian?'

He suddenly stopped in his tracks. He turned to face her, his hands on her shoulders, a frown on his lips. 'Mary. There is something I have wanted to say to you for a long time, but I fear I still do not have the words.'

Mary shivered. 'Surely there can be nothing so very dire between us, Lord Sebastian?'

'Perhaps not for you, Mary. Perhaps you do not recall it at all. But at our first meeting, I behaved like an intolerable lout and I have not been able to forgive myself.'

Mary tried to pull away from him, shaking her head. Of course she remembered; but she did not want to. Not now. Now seemed like a whole different life from then. 'Please,

Sebastian. That was so long ago and I was just a foolish girl. I hope I have learned more of the game of flirtation now.'

He wouldn't let her go, his hands holding her with him. Making her face the past, as well as the present. 'No, you were not foolish at all. You were sweet and kind, and I was in a horrible sort of daze after losing my friends. I listened to the wrong people; I sought to forget my pain in the worst sort of way and I am sorry for it. Heartily sorry.'

Mary stared up at him, her head whirling. She had imagined just such a scene when she was younger, Sebastian apologising to her. She had imagined herself gracious and majestic, forgiving him. And she did forgive him, but she did not feel at all majestic. Indeed, she wanted to cry.

She didn't know what to say, what to feel. She wanted so much to believe his solemn words, believe he had changed, as she had, but she was also afraid.

'I know you cannot truly forgive me,' he said. 'But I wanted you to know. I needed you to know. And also to know that I will always stand as your friend.'

Her friend. Of course. Despite the wonder of their kisses, that was all they could be. She might have started to think more of him, want more, since they first met in London, but what if she was wrong? She slowly nodded and tried to smile at him.

There was a burst of trumpets sounding from the terrace behind them. She turned towards the sound, glad of the distraction, of the moment when she did not yet have to examine her feelings.

The royal family had emerged from the ballroom, apparently intending to process on the beach. Their satins and brocades sparkled in the night. Mary caught a glimpse of Teresa, carrying the edge of Doña Carlota's train. She remembered her friend's flash of fear on their carriage ride, the secrets that had seemed to flicker in Teresa's eyes before she laughed.

So many secrets here. She did not know where to turn.

She looked back to Sebastian and found he did not watch the royal party, but still studied her.

She hoped desperately that she *could* trust him now, because she didn't know who else to turn to and she feared for her father. 'You asked what else we ladies talk about on our long, dull days.'

He blinked, as if surprised. But he quickly recovered, giving her a puzzled half-smile. 'And what is that?'

'Families, of course.' She gestured to the glittering group making its stately way along the terrace. Dom Joao and his wife did not touch, did not even look at each other. 'None are surely quite as convoluted as the Braganzas, I am sure.'

'What do you mean?'

Mary hesitated. 'I am friends with a lady-in-waiting to the Princess and she fears Doña Carlota is not at all happy about her new life in Brazil. That perhaps she hopes to recreate some of the coterie she enjoyed in Lisbon. That she perhaps will make some trouble if she does not get her way.'

Sebastian went tense at her side. 'Did your friend say what manner of trouble that might be?'

Mary shook her head. 'It was only hints. But

surely it is no secret Doña Carlota does not care for her husband? That she, and many of her friends, would do much to return to Europe? If there is trouble—I do fear for my father's safety. He has risked so much to bring about this relocation.'

'What can I do to help you, Mary? I do not know of any plots and if I did...'

'You could not tell me. I know that. I just— will you help keep my father safe? If you truly wish to make amends to me. I do worry about him.'

'Of course I will. I admire your father a great deal and we all must keep each other safe here.'

'Thank you,' Mary said, reassured by his quiet, solemn words.

'Mary!' Teresa called from the edge of the terrace.

Mary glanced back to see her friend waving. Teresa smiled, but Mary could see the tension on her face. 'I must go now,' she said quickly. 'But I do thank you, Sebastian, truly. You will not be sorry for helping me and my father.'

'Mary,' he called as she turned away. 'If your friend is Teresa Fernandes…'

'I have many friends,' she said carelessly.

'Of course. But her brother…'

'Luis?'

'Yes. You should be rather careful of him, you know. He has long been associated with many of Doña Carlota's old friends.'

Mary swallowed hard. She remembered Luis's flirtations, his laughter—but also the dark looks she could not quite explain, the flicker on Teresa's face when she said her brother's name. 'He and his sister have been most welcoming to me since I came to Portugal.'

'And there is no need for you to shun them; quite the contrary. But you yourself said there was much danger everywhere here. Everyone has their own plans, their own desires.'

'Mary!' Teresa called again. 'Have you heard? The countess is giving another party tomorrow, a picnic. Doesn't that sound lovely?'

'Lovely indeed, Teresa!' Mary gave Sebastian a quick nod. 'I will be careful, of course.'

She hurried away, dashing up the steps of

the terrace just in time to see the royal party turn the corner amid their trumpets and satins. She looked back, but Sebastian had vanished into the night. Leaving only darkness.

You will not be sorry...

Sebastian hurried to the other end of the terrace, where he could watch the royal couple as they processed with their courtiers, where he could see Mary return to her friends. That was certainly where she was quite wrong, for he was already sorry. If he was to help her now, help keep her safe from what was happening around them, then he would have to spend more time with her. Time watching her, hearing her laughter, seeing her sweet smile. And then how would he stop himself from kissing her again?

Right when he had promised himself he would never hurt her like that again.

When he'd looked at her tonight, the moonlight silvery on her delicate face, the compassion in her eyes as he told her the pitiful truth of what had happened in London, it took everything in his power, every ounce of all the self-control he had learned in the last few years, not to grab her in his arms. Not to pull her close and kiss her lovely pink lips, feel her warmth yielding against him.

He was so desperate to kiss her again—Mary Manning, of all women! Mary, who always watched him with such well-earned suspicion.

But he wanted to be a better man now, better for her, because of her. To do that he had to do his job there in Brazil, had to keep her from being hurt by matters she had no part in making.

He saw her meet her friend Teresa Fernandes on the terrace, saw them whisper in each other's ears. Mary laughed, her cheeks flushed pink in the torchlight. She glanced around them, but he knew she could not see him there in the shadows.

He glimpsed Nicholas Warren at the edges of the crowd and noticed his friend also watched the two women, his eyes wide with admiration for Senhorita Fernandes. Sebastian couldn't help fearing for their mission if everyone involved was lovesick!

He had to be on his guard, now more than ever.

As if to prove he was right in thinking that, there was a sudden popping sound from the trees at the edge of the terrace. At first, it seemed like nothing, like the merest ruffling in the breeze, but then it rang out again, louder, and he realised it was a gun firing. He spun around to make sure Mary was in the villa and saw the Princess's ladies dashing into the house, shrieking. Princess Carlota stood still, her head held defiantly high, even as her own ladies fled. Mary was nowhere to be seen.

Sebastian ran into the garden, along with some of the royal guards, their own firearms held high. Yet there was nothing there at all— just a lingering sense that even the paradise of a Brazilian jungle couldn't hold the world at bay.

Mary took her father's hand and let him help her up into their carriage. She had tried to stop Teresa from finding her father and telling him Mary was feeling unwell, and had tried to stop her father from leaving the party, but now she had to admit she was glad of his silent, comfortable presence at her side, of the darkness and warmth of their carriage. After the noise of the party, the whirl of her own thoughts with Sebastian, it helped to be able to take a deep breath.

She peeked out the window as her father turned back to say something to one of his secretaries. The house was still lit up like a torch in the dusty dark blue of the tropical night and she could hear the faint strains of music as the party went on. Surely Sebastian was still in there as well. Was he dancing with someone else?

She turned away sharply from the sight of the house and smoothed her glove over her wrist. Suddenly she glimpsed something in the shadows, a flash of something white on the seat across from her. She knew it had not been there before and her heart pounded as she reached for it.

It was a small, folded scrap of cheap paper. Scrawled across it in pencil were a few words addressed to 'Senhor Manning'.

Your interference in the affairs of Portugal is not welcome. You have been

warned before. Now you must leave the
governance of the royal crown to those
who claim it as their right. This is your
final warning.

Shocked, Mary read over the note again.
Surely she must be dreaming those words! Her
father was devoted to his duty. What could
such a thing mean?

She suddenly remembered all Sebastian's
warnings, which had made her feel so frus-
trated with him, and with herself that she could
not decode them. Was this what he meant?

The door to the carriage opened again and
her father sat down beside her. She quickly
tried to slip the note into her reticule, but he
saw her do that and laughed. 'Is it a love letter, my dear?'

'I—no. Of course not,' Mary answered,
wishing her voice did not shake so much.

William frowned. 'What is it, then? Something unpleasant?'

He took it from her and quickly scanned the
note. She watched his face carefully, but his

expression did not change. He merely shrugged and crumpled the paper in his gloved hand.

'Do not let such things worry you, Mary,' he said.

'How can I not let such things worry me?' she cried. 'It says you have received such warnings before.'

'Everyone in diplomatic service gets such messages from time to time,' he said. He tapped on the door, and the carriage lurched into motion, leaving the party behind.

Mary had been eager to escape, but now she wasn't so sure. The thick trees of the jungle road looked too dark and empty now. 'Should we not have brought servants with us, then?'

'I certainly would, if I feared for *your* safety, my dear,' he said. He patted her hand and smiled. 'But we have known all along that not everyone in the royal court favoured coming to Brazil. They can do nothing to us now that we are here, not really, and they know it. These are cheap theatrics and I want you to think no more of them.'

Mary studied his face carefully, trying to see beyond the reassuring smile he always gave her. She didn't want him to worry about her, so she smiled in return. But she vowed to herself to be more vigilant in the future—and to brave a conversation with Sebastian again, to find out exactly what he had meant by his warnings.

Chapter Eighteen

⟨⟨⟨⟩⟩⟩

The next day was the countess's promised picnic and Mary's father had insisted she attend, even as she would rather stay with him and keep watch over him. It was a beautiful, sun-filled day, but she couldn't quite be rid of the cold, disquieting feeling that had kept her awake last night. She had wandered away from the crowd for a moment, hoping for a quiet space to think.

Mary turned to look over her shoulder at the Countess de Graumont's villa, cradled in the small valley below the hillside where the guests had wandered to gather tropical berries. It was not large, but lovely, like a fairy-tale house with its white walls and blue-tiled roof, the figures of the picnic guests dotted through the dark green of the trees like pale ghosts. Laughter and chatter floated to her on the breeze, as if the brief drama of the mysterious gunshots had never happened at all.

She knew she should be down there with them, but she loved the quiet moment, floating above everything. The moment to think. Ever since she had arrived on Brazil's sandy shore, it had felt like a new world, a place where she didn't quite understand everything that happened around her. It was like no place else she had ever known; *she* was unlike she had ever been. She suddenly wanted to run and laugh, to inhale every sweet, flowery, sea salt scent on every breeze.

Was it Brazil's fault? Or was it Sebastian?

Mary frowned. She thought of him far too much, this man she had once tried so hard to forget. Yet he seemed so tied up in this place, so tied up in the Mary she was only just discovering.

She found a tiny, silver-satin ribbon of a stream, running between the towering stands of coconut trees, and followed its meandering twists and turns up hills and around boulders until it grew wider, running faster, darker. Soon she couldn't see the picnic-goers any longer; the dark greenery, the thick, humid air, the rolling grey clouds overhead had closed in around her and she felt a cold touch of surprise at being so very alone.

Or not so very alone after all. She heard the echo of a voice, loud but faraway, and an answer, a shout. She crept to the top of one of the boulders and peeked over.

On the opposite bank of the stream, she could see a small group of about four men. Two of them were obviously confronting each other about something, one of them shouting, the other holding up his hands. The shouting man pushed the other and his hat fell off so that Mary could see with a start that it was Luis Fernandes. Who were the other men and what could Teresa's brother be quarrelling with them about?

A loud crash of thunder overhead jerked her back to the present moment. She spun around, her heart pounding, and saw nothing behind her at all but the trees. She had surely gone much further than she intended, much further than she should have. When she turned back, Luis and the others had vanished and she wondered if she had imagined them.

She clambered down the slope to the banks of the stream, hoping it would lead her back to the villa. But as she reached the edge of the water, a sudden, sharp fork of lightning split the grey sky above her head, making her jump. The blue-silver sizzle lit the swaying tops of the palm trees above her and brought a chilly wind sweeping down from the dark hills. The sharp, sulphurous smoke bit at her throat, and she was suddenly deeply aware of how alone she was in a strange place.

Then the clouds split and the heavy rain dashed down to the earth.

It was surprisingly cold and needle-like, pelting against her skin through her thin spencer jacket, and she gasped. She spun around, trying to find her way, and nearly slipped on the mud beneath her. For a second, she feared she would fall into the stream.

'Mary! What are you doing out here?' she heard someone shout over the roar of the rain.

Warm, hard hands caught at her shoulders,

swinging her around. It was Sebastian, solid and strong, anchoring her in the storm.

Mary stared up at him. The thick, bright waves of his hair were darkened by the rain, slicked back to give his chiselled face an austere beauty. The raindrops landed on the tips of his eyelashes, sparkling like tiny diamonds.

She curled her chilled hands into the front of his coat. 'Did you see them over there?' she gasped.

His glance darted swiftly over her head. 'Did you come out here following someone? Your friend Senhorita Fernandes said she lost sight of you at the picnic, she was worried you had been gone for some time.'

'I—no,' she answered doubtfully. She couldn't see anyone on the opposite bank now at all. It seemed she and Sebastian were alone in the grey mist of the world. 'I just wandered too far, I think. It's so beautiful out here, or was before the rain. Were you just here looking for me?'

He gave a wry laugh and didn't quite answer her. 'We must get you out of the rain, before you catch the ague.'

He bent down and caught her under her knees, swinging her up into his arms. Mary was so surprised by his sudden movement, overcome by the dizzying moment, the rain, the smell of the greenery and the distant sea, that she could make no protest. His body was so warm and strong, so alive. She wished that moment could just go on and on, could be frozen for an instant.

But she feared *she* would be the one to freeze first. The rain made her shiver and she held on tightly to Sebastian as he carried her up the slope of a hill, into the shelter of a shallow cave.

The rage of the storm was suddenly silent, muffled by the damp stone walls, the pebbled, sandy floor.

'It's not much,' Sebastian said as he lowered her to her feet. 'But it's home. For now, anyway.' He held on to her arm until she was steady again and then he would have stepped back, but Mary caught his arm.

'They *were* there, weren't they?' she said. 'Those men. I know I did not imagine them.'

Sebastian seemed to hesitate and Mary's

hand tightened on his arm. His eyes were so dark as he looked down at her, his body so tense. 'Please,' she said. 'Please, trust me. I fear I cannot quite trust myself. I want to know…'

But her words ended as his lips swooped down on hers, catching her breath, her senses, everything but the thought of *him*.

With a low moan, she wound her arms around his neck and held him close to her. She had tried to force away her feelings for him, yet they would not be banished. Those feelings burst free now, leaping free under his kiss.

'Oh, no, Mary,' he whispered. 'It's I who cannot trust myself. Not when I'm with you.'

Chapter Nineteen

Mary had never been in a more magical place.

Even though in reality it was merely a small cave, surrounded by towering palms, in the faint, flickering rainy light it seemed like an enchanted spot, full of ancient spirits.

'Mary, I…' he began again, his voice hoarse.

Mary shook her head. She didn't want anything to break that wondrous spell that seemed to wrap around them there, holding them safely together against the dangers that lay beyond. She was done with the worry she had been carrying since they last met in London. She was no longer the same person she was back then and neither was he. The bright-green eyes that looked down at her now were no longer clouded by the secrets he had carried back then.

She pressed her finger to his lips to hold his words at bay. He looked back at her, his eyes narrowed with desire.

She stepped back to unfasten her jacket and slipped it from her shoulders. She stared deeply into his eyes, holding that connection between them like a silk scarf, as she drew down the deep, drawstring neckline of her muslin dress. She was most grateful for the simpler, lighter styles of the tropics, which let her do such a thing before she could think about it too much. Before she could let fear stop her from leaping forward again. From truly living.

He watched her, his attention never wavering, his whole body still and tense. She could read nothing in the bright-green glow of his eyes. She swallowed hard and forced herself to look back at him. What if she was going about this all wrong? What if…?

What if he turned away from her and what she offered, as he had in London? A sudden cold fear threatened to sweep away the warmth of the night around them.

No! She pressed away the fear. This was right now, she could feel it deep down inside.

When he had told her about his family on the beach, when he swept her up into his arms just now, fear and protectiveness in his eyes, she had known it was different now.

He reached out and she saw that his hand shook slightly. Somehow that reassured her. His fingers touched her hair, softly, gently.

She leaned her cheek into his palm, revelling in the way it felt.

'Mary,' he groaned. 'You are so very beautiful.'

'I feel beautiful—with you,' she answered. She went up on tiptoe to press her lips to his cheek, his neck. She felt the warmth of his skin, felt the sharp breath he drew in.

'You keep me safe now, I know it,' she whispered. 'I want you to kiss me, to touch me. Don't you—don't you want me, too? When you kissed me at the masked ball...'

'Of course I want you, lovely Mary. I have wanted you for so long, and I—heaven help me, I can't hold it back any longer!' His words vanished as his lips covered hers, hard and hungry, no longer to be denied. His hands slid over her bare shoulders, hard and strong.

Mary wrapped her arms around him, holding him close. It was as if some force, kept imprisoned deep inside for far too long, broke free and swept them both away, like the tides of the ocean far below their hiding place.

That force guided her as she unwrapped his cravat and pushed his soft linen shirt away from his chest. Her fingertips slid over his bare skin and she was fascinated by the new, forbidden sensation of it. The heat of his body seemed to seep into her very soul and in that moment she only knew *him*.

Sebastian moaned deep in his throat and he swept her up into his arms. Twined together, they tumbled down on to the cloak spread on the sandy ground beneath them. The palm trees and the moon in the dusty black sky beyond the opening of their shelter whirled dizzily over her head.

Mary laughed, giddy with the joy of the moment, and landed atop him. She drew back to look down at him, his face gilded in the night light. He was so beautiful, she could scarcely breathe. So wondrously golden and alive.

With one trembling finger, she traced the

light, coarse blond hair sprinkled across his lean chest, the thin line that led tantalisingly to the band of his buff breeches. He watched her, not moving, letting her explore as if he sensed that was what she needed to do.

His stomach muscles tightened, his breath catching as her touch brushed over him.

'Mary—' he gasped again '—I have waited so long. But you must be very sure, too.'

'I am,' was all she could say. She could barely breathe.

Sebastian arched up to catch her in his arms, his mouth claiming hers again. There was nothing careful, nothing held back in that kiss, it was all urgent need bursting into the sky like fireworks.

She felt the rough slide of his hands over her back as he untied the back of her gown. The night sea breeze was warm on her skin, but it was as nothing next to his touch. She shrugged the muslin away, delighting in the sudden feeling of freedom, in the way he looked at her, as if she was something precious.

'My Mary,' he said. He wrapped his arms

around her and rolled her beneath him, into the softness of their pile of discarded clothes.

Mary laughed as her hair tumbled around them. She felt so wondrously free in his arms! The past was gone; there was only now. He kissed her and all other thoughts vanished.

She closed her eyes, letting herself fall deeply into his touch, his kiss. As his mouth touched her bare shoulder, the curve of her breast, she slid her palms down the bare length of his back. He moved over her, his body strong against the night.

Her legs parted as his hips leaned into her and she felt the hardness of his manhood behind the thin fabric of his breeches. She knew what that meant, what would happen. She'd heard married ladies whisper about it in drawing rooms across Europe. Her own mother had given her a book about 'marital relations' years ago. But none of those frantic descriptions hinted at how it all *felt*. Of that dizzy sensation of falling, falling, but in another person.

'Mary,' he whispered against her shoulder. 'I need you as I have never needed anything in my life. But I don't want to hurt you. Never again.'

She smiled, feeling how he held himself back. But she didn't want him to do that any more; never again. 'You can't hurt me, Sebastian, I know it.'

Boldly, she spread her legs a bit wider, invitingly, beneath him. She felt him reach between them to unfasten his breeches and then he was pressed against her.

She closed her eyes, concentrating on the feeling as he carefully eased inside her. There was a small pain, a burning, as she had read there would be, but it was nothing compared to the way it felt to be truly joined with him.

She arched up closer against him, wrapping her arms and legs around him so tightly that the moment could never end.

Slowly, he moved again within her, sliding back inch by enticing inch, then driving forward, a little deeper, a little more intimate every time. To her surprise, a warm, delightful feeling caught at her and spread over her body, like the Brazilian sun.

'Sebastian...' She gasped. Behind her closed

eyes, brilliant lights flashed, that heat grew and grew. How could she bear it, without being consumed in him?

Above her, all around her, she felt Sebastian's body grow tense. His breath was warm against her skin and his head arched back.

'Mary!' he shouted out and she felt that heat shatter, consuming her. She clung on to him, feeling as if they tumbled down together into the flames.

After long, brittle, still moments that could have been days, or mere seconds, Mary slowly opened her eyes. To her surprise, they were still in the mountain clearing, the palm trees looming beyond, the silvery light of the moon filtering down in flickering shadows.

Yet everything seemed entirely new. Life had a new—sparkle about it. Thanks to Sebastian.

Mary found she felt too heavy, too deliciously exhausted, to move. She turned her head on their makeshift bed to look at Sebastian in the moonlight. His eyes were closed, his limbs sprawled in answering exhaustion, but his face looked peaceful, younger, a small smile on his beautiful lips.

She smiled in answer and closed her eyes to feel his warmth against her, the soft, flower-scented breeze floating over them. His arm came heavy over her waist, drawing her closer into the angles of his body.

'Mary,' he whispered against her hair. 'I can't pretend to even begin to understand you, but I find I do know one thing.'

Mary laughed. 'And what is that?'

'That you are the sweetest, most forgiving of maddening ladies.'

She rolled over to face him. The sparkling moonlight outlined his handsome, sharply chiselled features, casting shadowy angles over his brow, his tumbled hair. She traced her fingertips over them carefully, as if she could memorise him. As if she could make him, and herself, brand new.

Mary sat up reluctantly and reached for her discarded dress. The light beyond their hiding place was growing paler and she knew soon they would be missed. They had to find out what had happened out there in the real world, beyond their dreams. 'Is it safe to return now, do you think?'

Sebastian rolled away and plucked up his own clothes. His face, so peaceful only moments before, now looked taut and serious. She could almost see his thoughts shoot beyond her, beyond this moment.

'We should go back, before we are missed,' he said. 'I must talk to people, find out what has happened. But I admit—I wish we did not have to leave quite yet. This place seems enchanted.'

Mary smiled, happy beyond reason that he felt something like she did. That they would have this moment to hold on to, no matter what happened. 'This whole place is enchanted. I vow I feel like a different person here. I have no fear.'

'Not *too* different, I hope,' he said teasingly. 'I rather like the old Mary.' His head bent towards hers and his lips touched hers, tender and sweet, a moment she wished could last for ever. He held her close and pressed a kiss to her hair before he let her go.

'But what is it I must fear?' she asked. He

took her hand and led her to the edge of their clearing. He kept her behind him as he looked around cautiously into the seemingly empty night. 'I have kept watch, as you warned me at the masked ball, but I have heard nothing except gossip. My friend Teresa seems worried, but she will not confide in me. Are she and her brother in some danger? Did they have something to do with what happened tonight?'

'My dear Mary,' he said urgently. 'Please believe me—I will keep you safe. I know you have no reason to trust me yet, but I will show you, very soon. Will you wait for me?'

Mary slowly nodded. 'I will wait—for a time.'

'Then that is all I can ask for. For now...'

Chapter Twenty

'Please, I must speak to Senhorita Fernandes! It is most urgent,' Mary begged the stone-faced footman who guarded the closed front doors of the royal palace.

'What does this regard, *senhorita*?' he asked. 'The ladies are with Her Royal Highness right now and should not be disturbed. It is the siesta hour.'

Mary glanced back over her shoulder at the plaza. It seemed rather early for any kind of 'siesta'. She had left the house as soon after breakfast as she could, right after her father left for his own work, and the square was crowded with people coming and going from the market. Native Brazilians in their pale cottons and bright jewellery mingled with Portuguese ladies and their maids, coming out of the church with their lace mantillas catching at the cool morning breeze. Soon it would be warm and people would indeed be seeking shelter, but surely not yet?

She hadn't been able to sleep with going over every dramatic moment of the day before. Because she knew she could not yet solve the puzzle of Sebastian, and her feelings for him, she had realised she had to work on what she *could* discover—what sort of treachery was afoot in the royal court and what her friend might have to do with it.

Mary took a deep breath and plunged past the footman, rushing as fast as she could down the corridor. 'Thank you very much! I will just look for myself, won't take a moment.'

'*Senhorita*, you cannot do that!' the footman cried. He hurried after her, but Mary was ahead of him.

She remembered that Teresa had mentioned her chamber was towards the back of the palace, small and dark, and she turned in what she hoped was that direction. She ran down narrow, twisting corridors that had obviously been cobbled together when the buildings were hastily connected to make the new palace, past closed doors and small sitting rooms crowded with people lazily fanning themselves and whispering together. They glanced up in faint interest as she ran past, but no one pursued her.

At last, she glimpsed Teresa at the end of one of the dim hallways. Teresa held a scrap of paper in her hand, frowning as she stared down at it, seeming to not notice anything around her.

'Teresa!' Mary called, hurrying towards her friend.

Teresa spun around, her eyes wide. She thrust the scrap of paper up the cuff of her long, tight sleeve. 'Mary! What are you doing here?'

'I told the *senhorita* it was not the time for calls,' the pursuing footman huffed.

'I must speak to you, Teresa, most urgently,' Mary insisted.

'It is quite all right,' Teresa told the servant. She smiled, hiding her worry behind the pale mask of her expression, and took Mary's arm.

'Come, my friend, walk with me. Are you ill? Can I help you?'

'No, no, I am quite well,' Mary assured her. 'But I hope that we can help each other.'

'Oh?' Teresa said. Her voice was quiet, but tense, quite unlike her usual merriness. She led Mary into a window embrasure, a small space shadowed and apart from the rest of the crowded palace. She stared out the window, to the crowd moving below with their market baskets. 'What is amiss?'

Mary was quite astonished Teresa would try to hide things, even now. 'What of what happened in the hills, at the countess's villa?'

Teresa bit her lip. 'When you vanished for a time?'

'After shots were fired? Surely that is not a usual thing at the Portuguese court?'

Teresa's face crumpled. 'I did not know such a thing would happen! Not yet, not—'

'Not yet?' Mary cried. 'Teresa, is something amiss? Perhaps something with Doña Carlota—or your brother? I can help you, if you will let me. I have been warned to beware, but how can I do that if I don't know what is happening?'

Teresa shook her head. She peeked out beyond their little sanctuary and quickly took Mary's hands in hers. 'I do not want any harm to come to you! You have been a good friend to me, my only real friend since my parents died, I think.'

'And you have been my friend, Teresa,' Mary whispered. 'Please, what is happening? Do you know who fired those shots in the hills?'

'I do not, I promise that is the truth. But my brother—he will do anything to get back to Europe, as will many others. They did not want to come to Brazil in the first place and thought we would only be here a short time. Now that it looks like it will be indefinite…'

'They would even talk to the French to get their place back?'

'I don't know. I know Luis wants to go home, very much. He gets more and more secretive, he asks me to find out things from Doña Carlota, but he will not tell me everything. I have become frightened of him.'

There was a sudden burst of laughter from the corridor, and Teresa closed her eyes. Her hands tightened on Mary's. 'We can't talk here. Find me at the Baroness Huelgos's ball tomorrow, yes? I will find out more before then. But you must be careful.'

Mary quickly nodded. It was clear she would find out no more from Teresa now. 'And you. Promise me.'

'Of course. I am always careful.' Teresa gave a strained little laugh, and slipped out of the window embrasure. Mary heard her join the group strolling past and their voices faded as they moved further down the corridor.

Mary peeked out to make sure no one was there before she, too, hurried on her way. But she couldn't leave the palace now that she was in, not quite yet. She hurried up a staircase towards the main drawing rooms.

It was definitely not one of the grander streets of Rio.

Sebastian nudged aside a pile of rubbish with the toe of his boot. The narrow lane was cobbled, but this area had not been one of the places hastily refurbished for the royal family's arrival. The stones were cracked, mouldy, and the lane was close-packed with buildings whose whitewash was peeling and grey. Lattice-covered balconies loomed overhead, which in daytime would surely cut off any meagre light that tried to slip past.

From behind those flimsy walls he could hear shrieks of laughter, noisy quarrels. The warm air was thick and humid, full of the scents of cooking fires, cheap perfumes and rotting garbage. It was after midnight, the hour of disreputable revels, but surely it would be no different at midday here.

It was far from the main square, from the palace and the cathedral, from the houses commandeered for the court. Was his informant correct in saying their quarry would be found meeting there?

He paused at the end of the lane to study the dwelling opposite. This was the place where his informant, a footman at the palace who was half-English, had said Luis Fernandes and his young, wild cohorts had been meeting. Sebastian settled in to wait in the shadows, his arms crossed over his chest, invisible in the shadows in his black garments. In this work, just as much as in battle, cool patience and forethought was a necessity to win the day, though not terribly glamorous.

He thought about Mary. Part of his task there in Rio was to keep her safe now. He was afraid he wasn't making a very good job of it so far. In fact, his desire for her, his need to have her, had only made matters worse. He had to fix that now.

A tiny, flickering light appeared in one of the cracked upper windows of the house he watched.

Sebastian crept across the lane, drawing a small but lethally sharp dagger from beneath his sleeve. Holding it balanced on his leather-gloved palm, he made his way to the half-concealed back door. It faced on to an alleyway even narrower than the front street, barely wide enough for one man to walk down. The tip of his knife made quick work of the flimsy lock.

The corridor inside was dark and dank, smelling of mould. From the upper floors, he could hear the indistinct, low murmur of voices. Moving quickly, silently, he made his way up a rickety staircase. He went past the half-open door of the room where the light flickered, where voices could be heard, louder for a moment, then muffled by the paint-flaked walls again. The heavy smell of rum combined with the sickly-sweetness of the mould.

He could not stop there. At the top of the narrow house, he found a narrow space under the eaves, just as his informant had said. It smelled dusty, as if nothing had disturbed the space for a long time. There was a small gap in the floorboards there, where he could peer down at a corner of the lighted room.

He glimpsed Luis Fernandes's profile, along with a couple of other young men of the royal court, men who were known to have been reluctant to leave their home—and who had been part of Doña Carlota's circle for a long time. They sat around a table laden with cigars and jugs of cheap local rum, and they were laughing.

'…won't be long now,' one of them said.

'But you did not do what you said you would up in the hills,' Luis said.

The man beside him scowled. 'The Princess said her husband would be there and when he was not...'

'Yes, yes,' Luis said impatiently. 'But we cannot stay in this godforsaken place much longer. The French will have overrun everything in Lisbon, taken all the spots of authority and left none for us, if we are not there to claim them. We must move.'

'But when? Dom Joao is always surrounded by the English now. He will listen to no one else.'

'You know we cannot count on him at all. The Princess will lead us back to Lisbon, will seek help from her Spanish family, who will make peace with Napoleon,' Luis said. 'We only need to go where she cannot now, to help her.'

'And where is that?' one of the other men said, his voice slurred as if they had been drinking the rum for too long.

Luis laughed, an unpleasant, humourless sound. 'To the centre of the English party, of course...'

Chapter Twenty-One

'Lord Sebastian Barrett has come to call on you, *senhorita*,' Adriana announced, a smile on her lips like the cat who had found the cream. She always did say Mary needed more gentleman callers, especially of an ilk as handsome as Lord Sebastian.

'Lord Sebastian?' Mary cried. It had been two days since she last saw Sebastian, in their hidden tropical bower. He had sent her a note and a bouquet of brilliant Brazilian flowers, but the note had been maddeningly vague. He hadn't been far from her thoughts, as she wondered where he was, what his work was and when she could tell him about her visit to the royal palace.

Now the daylight was fading outside her

window, and she was thinking of changing her gown for the night's ball at the Huelgos villa outside the city. She still wore her plain afternoon gown. It was not the expected hour for calls.

Yet Mary's heart pounded at the sound of his name and she had to hold herself back from running downstairs to see his face, to know he was really there. She had to be much more careful to conceal her real feelings this time.

Adriana giggled behind her apron. 'Indeed. He seemed most eager to see you, *senhorita*.'

Mary quickly tidied her hair and hurried down the stairs. Her father had already departed, brushing off her worries that he looked tired, and the house was quiet. Sebastian was pacing the drawing-room floor, his cravat loosened, his hair windswept. He was surely the most handsome sight she had ever seen.

Even more so when he turned to her with a smile.

'I hope I did not keep you waiting,' Mary said. She wished desperately that her voice did not sound so eager, so breathless.

'Not at all, Miss Manning. I am sorry to call at such an inconvenient hour.'

He hurried across the room to take her hand and he bowed over it in a most polite manner. It did not feel so very *polite*, though. The brush of his lips over her skin made her shiver.

'Please, do sit down,' Mary said, somewhat flustered. She quickly covered it up, and led him to one of the sofas near the window, just beyond the golden-pink light of the dying sun. He sat down near her, his leg warm through her skirt.

'I am so happy to see you again, Mary, and looking so—well,' he said.

Mary smiled at him shyly. 'I know you must be very busy lately.'

'So I have been, but I have thought so much of—' Sebastian broke off and shook his head. 'Mary, are you going to the ball tonight?'

She was confused by the sudden question, unsure of what she had really been expecting from him. 'Of course.' She tried to laugh, even though the solemn look in his eyes made her feel rather apprehensive. 'Shall I save you a dance there?'

He smiled. 'I will always want to dance with you, Mary. But I must warn you tonight to beware of your dance partners.'

'Beware?' Mary asked, even more confused. 'La, Sebastian, but you sound most foreboding!'

He gave a rueful laugh. 'I hope I am not such a Minerva Press novel. But we have lately discovered a few—facts about some of the Portuguese courtiers. It could be a dangerous moment soon.'

Mary thought of what she had found at the royal palace, of Teresa's fear, and she was tired of never knowing. Of always being kept 'safe', by her father and now by Sebastian. It was maddening, the way they would never tell her anything! 'Facts about Doña Carlota and her French friends?'

Sebastian studied her closely. 'Perhaps, yes.'

His reticence, the lack of expression on his handsome face, suddenly made her rather angry. She had been working in this world for so long; surely she could be trusted to know the truth now, the full truth? Surely she could help?

Besides—she and Sebastian had been as intimate as two people could be. Why would he not talk to her freely now?

It made her doubt she could truly trust him once again.

'Sebastian, please,' she begged. 'If there is danger here...'

'You know you must be wary of Teresa Fernandes and her brother,' he said, but that was all. He glanced behind her, almost as if he thought they would be overheard.

Mary slid her hands out of his. 'You have said so before. But they have been kind to me and Teresa at least has surely never been dishonest with me. If she could help...'

'Mary, please,' he said, his voice low and tense. 'I can tell you no more, not yet. Just, please, be careful of them. Stay close to me or to your father tonight.'

Nothing had changed, she realised with a cold sinking in her heart. Not really. Not where it mattered. She stood up and turned away from him, too confused to look at him any longer. When they had made love, she had never felt so close to another person's feelings and needs, never been so sure of anything. Now she felt like a fool for him all over again.

'I must change for the evening, Lord Sebastian,' she said carefully. 'Thank you for your warning. I will be most careful, as always.'

'Mary...' he said, his tone verging on angry, impatient. But he just took a deep breath and gave her a polite smile. He kissed her hand once more, but she could not bear the feelings his touch raised in her. 'Look for me at the ball. I will be watching for you.'

She nodded and heard him leave the room, Adriana fluttering after him to the front door. When she was sure he was gone, Mary ran up the stairs towards her own chamber. At the window on the turning of the stairs, she stopped and looked down at the street. Sebastian was just climbing into his carriage and she caught a glimpse of the dying sunlight on his hair.

Why could he not trust her, let her help him? She wanted so much to be sure of him again.

She slowly turned away and made her way into her chamber, where Adriana had laid out her silk ballgown and the jewellery parure of cameos and pearls that had been her mother's. It always made Mary feel more confident when she wore them, more sure of herself, as if her mother stood with her and helped her do her duty.

She could only hope the armour would help her tonight.

The music had already begun when Mary's carriage deposited her at the front doors of the hillside villa of the Baroness Huelgos, a long, low, pale structure lit up by thousands of candles in the warm, dusty dark night. She slowly made her way into the ballroom, looking for her father, or Sebastian, or anyone she knew. The sky felt lower, heavy, as if rain was moving in on their party.

She glimpsed Doña Carlota and some of her ladies seated on a dais at the far end of the room, but Teresa was not among them. Mary went up on tiptoe, trying to see over the heads of the crowd around her, but she could see little. She made her way to a quieter corner and glimpsed Teresa beside the tall windows lead-ing outside to the gardens. Teresa gave her a small wave, but her smile was strained.

Mary started to move towards her, when her hand was suddenly caught. She spun around, half-hoping it was Sebastian, only to find Luis smiling down at her.

'Senhorita Manning,' he said, bowing over her hand. He was as handsome as ever, as fashionably perfect in his dark evening dress, yet Mary was sure she saw something else in the depths of his charming, practised smile. 'How lovely you look tonight.'

'Thank you, Senhor Fernandes,' she said, giving him her own practised smile. Perhaps if she could get him to talk to her, she could learn something. If she could then make Sebastian listen to her…

But he would not talk to her and she felt alone in the crowded party. Alone with a man whose touch made her feel nothing like Sebastian's did.

'I have not seen you or Teresa much of late,' she said. 'I imagine you have been kept very busy with new duties here in Brazil.'

His eyes narrowed a bit as he looked down

at her. 'Yes, busy indeed, thanks to men like your father and his friends. But surely we are never too busy for *you*. Perhaps you would care to dance with me now?'

Mary glanced past him to see Teresa watching her, her eyes wide. Then her friend vanished behind a wall of pale-silk gowns. Mary remembered what Sebastian had said, but surely a dance would not harm anything?

'I would enjoy that, thank you,' she answered. She took his offered arm and let him lead her towards the dance floor. His muscles were tense beneath her light touch and up close she could see the taut lines at the edge of his smile. A few moist beads dotted his brow, even though the tall windows of the ballroom wafted a cool breeze from the night outside.

It made Mary feel tense, as well, and she looked around in hopes of glimpsing Sebastian at last. But he was nowhere to be seen.

As they took their places in the dance, she took a deep breath and said, 'I understand from Teresa you have long been very useful in the court of Doña Carlota.'

He smiled at her, a strange, taut, too-bright

smile. 'She is a great princess, though I fear often my fellow courtiers do not always know her full worth. If they had listened to her counsel…'

'Her counsel?'

'On the hasty removal from Portugal. I am afraid fear prevailed, rather than her own sensible view that a European monarch's place is in Europe. Now it will be much harder to fix matters.'

'Fix matters?' Mary said as they swirled and dipped in time to the music. His hold on her was too hard, but she did not know how to break away yet.

'Surely you cannot be as in the dark about the truth of things here in Brazil as you pretend, Senhorita Manning? Your father is a well-known diplomat, one of the architects of the plan to carry off Dom Joao to this godforsaken place and take over his rule. And you have been most friendly with Lord Sebastian Barrett, as well. I am sure you could tell us much—if you would.'

All Sebastian's warnings echoed in Mary's head. She could not look away from the glitter of Luis's eyes. 'My father does not confide in me, I fear. I would know little of what he said anyway.'

'Now, we know that is not true. Come, Senhorita Manning, we should be honest with each other at last.'

The music ended with a flourish and Mary spun around to leave the dance floor. Luis grabbed her arm in a hard grasp, holding her by his side. The chill of her earlier frustration with Sebastian was nothing to the sudden, icy prick of her fear now. She knew she shouldn't have danced with him, listened to him.

She tugged hard at her arm, but he held her tightly, dragging her with him to the edge of the crowd.

'You must listen to me,' he muttered close to her ear, all his old charm vanished in cold hardness.

'Let go of me!' Mary cried, attracting curious glances from a few of the dancers, but no one came closer. She tried to kick out at him, but her heavy silk skirts wrapped around her legs.

Then she felt a sharp prick against the bare

skin of her arm, just above the edge of her glove. She glanced down, shocked that he would do such a thing. He held a small but lethal-looking dagger pressed to her, a tiny bloom of blood staining the white glove.

'Don't make such a fuss, Senhorita Manning. We are friends, are we not?' Luis whispered. 'Just come with me for a short time, listen to me. It's very important that people like your father and your admirer Lord Sebastian listen to reason. The fate of so many depends on that. Once they do, you will be immediately released to their loving care.'

'You can't kill me here in front of so many of your own people,' Mary hissed.

'Perhaps not. But do you see my sister over there?' Luis gestured towards Teresa, who was glimpsed through the swirl of the crowd. A tall, broad-shouldered man Mary did not know held Teresa by the arm and Teresa looked up at him with wide eyes and a pale face, quite unlike her usual laughing merriness. 'You would not want *her* to be hurt either, would you?'

Mary swallowed hard and Teresa met her eyes. She shook her head.

Luis tugged hard on Mary's arm, throwing her off balance on her delicate slippers and dangerously near to the knife.

'My poor sister,' he said with a theatrical sigh. 'She has always been so admirable, too naïve in the world. Our parents told me to look after her, but she must know some things are more important. Napoleon cannot be resisted and Doña Carlota is the only one not foolish enough to think he can. Teresa protests now, but she won't when we're back in Lisbon and she is married to some French officer. But if she does not make it home because of her—mistaken friendships...'

Mary looked back frantically to Teresa, who was still held by the muscle-bound man.

'Are you threatening your own sister?' Mary gasped.

'Senhorita Manning! Unlike your own countrymen, who bullied their way into my country, I don't want to harm the innocent. But so much peril awaits those who are not careful—such as you and my sister. Some causes are larger than us all and sacrifices must be made. I hope you do see what I mean?'

Mary swallowed hard. Indeed she did—too well. Come with him, be bait to Sebastian, or this wild-eyed man could hurt her friend. His own sister.

He drew her with him out the doors and on to the terrace outside the house, beyond the lights and music. She had dangerously underestimated the deep divide here in Brazil between those who thought it best to stay in Brazil under British protection and those who wanted to return to Portugal, even under price of submitting to Napoleon. Perhaps she had been too distracted by her feelings for Sebastian, her own romantic dreams?

He pulled her down the steps, towards the narrow, winding path that led up into the hills where she and Teresa had explored only days before. He was too strong for her, lifting her off her feet. Panicked, she glanced back, but Luis was too fast, too determined. He had carried her far from the crowd. She could see no one, nothing at all in the growing darkness. There were only the wavering shadows of the wildness beyond the garden and the surge of the black sea below.

There was a sudden explosion overhead, the promised fireworks shattering in a thousand glittering ruby-and-emerald shards. In the burst of light, she glimpsed Luis's face, distorted beyond recognition.

She had a sudden thought, something from one of the novels they had read on the long voyage. She pulled off her necklace, her distinctive cameo on its thin gold chain. She dropped it on a low, flowering bush, praying that Sebastian would look for her, find it and realise she had not left the ball willingly. That she realised his warnings were all too real.

She stumbled deliberately at the edge of the gravelled walkway, trying to slow him down. Luis cursed and yanked her up roughly. Mary managed to step on the hem of her gown, tearing part of the lace flounce and leaving it behind as well.

'Damnable slow, *puta*,' Luis growled. 'Do you want to be the reason I'm forced to hurt my sister? Hurt you? I am not a monster.'

He yanked so hard on her arm that Mary cried out at the hot jolt of pain. 'I can hardly run! I'm wearing dance slippers. And why should I co-operate with a brute like you?'

'I said to shut up!' He swung around, and in a split second Mary saw his fist come up in a flashing, pale arc towards her jaw.

It was the last thing she saw before a burst of white lights—and then darkness.

The elaborate fireworks of the royal party had already begun when Sebastian arrived. He had intended to be there much earlier, to snatch a quiet moment with Mary, to make her see how he really felt about her, that he could not live without her any longer. That the past was gone and he had to make her see that.

A packet of delayed letters from London had reached his lodgings just as he tied his cravat. One of them had an account of some Doña Carlota's new dealings, some of her letters purloined before they could reach her Spanish family—doings that affected all the English in Brazil. He had to protect Mary even more now.

That knowledge lay on his mind heavily as he hurried up the steps of the Huelgos villa. The orchestra played a waltz as the fireworks shot overhead, their explosions almost drowning out the music. The faces of the crowd were turned up to watch, the sparkling lights gleaming on their jewels, their fine silks and gold embroidery. All the luxury seemed almost unreal after what he had read in the letters.

He did not see Mary among them.

'Lord Sebastian!' he heard a woman cry. He spun around to find Teresa Fernandes hurrying towards him though the crowd, not paying any attention to the protests around her as she bumped into them. Her dark hair was tousled, her cheeks bright pink, not her usual Continental elegance at all. He felt a surge of concern.

She grabbed his arm, her hand tight on his sleeve. 'Lord Sebastian, please, you must help. He will catch me again and Mary—Mary...'

'Senhorita Fernandes, please, you must slow down and tell me what has happened. I assure you, you are safe now. I have come to find Mary, but it seems she isn't here yet.'

She shook her head and sucked in a deep breath. 'My brother was so angry before we came to the ball. I didn't want to travel with him, but he insisted, he said he had to talk to his—his friends. I just saw him with Mary and then they were gone! As soon as I could get away, I ran outside to look for her, but I could see nothing. I found this...' She held out a shaking hand to show him a pendant on a broken gold chain. 'She was wearing it earlier.'

'Where exactly did you find it?' Sebastian demanded. The broken links looked as if they had been snapped and he couldn't help but envision them breaking around Mary's delicate neck. He clenched his fist, knowing he had to be cold, to get his anger under control if he was going to help her now. It was a battle, just like the ones he had faced as a soldier, but with even greater stakes.

'On the pathway that leads out of the garden, into the hills,' Teresa said, her voice thick. 'I fear my brother has been meeting some of his friends there, in some of the caves. They want to talk about finding a way back to Lisbon.'

A way back to Lisbon—even through the French. 'What else was she wearing?'

Teresa blinked hard, as if her mind was too full of fear to remember anything else. Then she shook her head hard. 'I— A pale silk gown. Blue, maybe? With lace flounces. So pretty. What if—oh, Lord Sebastian, I fear my brother is no longer in his right mind! He is being driven by the thought that his home has been stolen from him. What if he has hurt her? I knew he was planning something tonight. It is all my fault.'

'Senhorita Fernandes, you must help me now,' Sebastian said firmly. He saw Nicholas Warren through the crowd and waved him over. He came quickly, his freckled face full of concern for Senhorita Fernandes—and for what he also knew was happening in secret with the royal family. 'I am going now to search for her. Mr Warren will help you here, you must find Miss Manning's father and have him put together a search party from here. I promise, I will find her and keep her safe.'

Teresa nodded, swallowing hard. 'I am sorry, Lord Sebastian.'

He left her with Nicholas, and hurried out the garden pathway where Teresa said the necklace had been found. There was nowhere Luis Fernandes could hide from him. And if anything had happened to Mary, he knew there was no place where he could hide from *himself.* He had put her in danger, not kept her safe enough, when he knew what was happening behind the scenes here in Rio.

But he would find her now and make sure no one hurt her again.

Chapter Twenty-Two

~~~~~~~~~~~~~~~~~~~~~~~~~~~~~~~~

Mary slowly blinked her eyes open. They felt gritty and heavy, as if glued down, and for an instant she couldn't remember anything. She could just feel a cold hardness beneath her, chilling through her thin gown.

She sat up slowly, carefully holding her head between her hands, which were bound in a light cord. To her shock, she found that she was stretched out on a stone floor covered with a layer of sand, her silk skirt streaked with dirt, her bare arms cold and aching, as if bruised. Images flashed through her mind—fireworks, gold and green in the night; swirling dancers; Teresa across the room, her face written with desperation.

Then it all came back to her, like that burst

of light from the fireworks. Luis had kidnapped her from the ball. He had knocked her unconscious and brought her to this place. But where was she? What had he hoped to achieve from such a desperate act?

She felt so dizzy, her head aching and throbbing. She blinked her eyes, trying to erase those flashing lights so she could study her surroundings. It was very dark around her, the only light a filter of moonlight from an opening high above her head, but gradually she could make out rough stone walls that pressed close around her. It looked like a cave, surely one of the looming structures she had glimpsed on her carriage drive with Teresa.

She shivered with a sudden jolt of fear, but she pushed it away, determined to get away. She seemed to be alone now, surrounded by silence, and she had to use that time.

Mary pushed herself carefully to her feet, swaying dizzily. She held her breath, wondering wildly if Luis still lurked there somewhere in the darkness? Would he hit her again? Worse—what if she couldn't find her way out of that place?

She forced that panic away. Fear would get her nowhere. She had to stay calm, assess the situation in a rational manner. She had watched her father do that for years when faced with diplomatic crises.

She knew she had to get away, to find Teresa and make sure her friend was safe, to warn her father and Sebastian. That thought gave her a renewed burst of strength. Yes, she had to find Sebastian. First, she had to free her hands. She quickly found a stony, sharp protrusion on the wall and rubbed the cords against it until they frayed enough to free her. There were small cuts on her skin, but she pushed away the sting.

She took another few steps, then was able to push herself faster. She made out the stone walls around her, which narrowed, then became wider, stone pillars rising in the distance.

Finally, she caught a glimpse of a faint gleam of light in the distance, brighter than the starlight from the opening overhead. She rushed towards it, hoping desperately it was not some kind of mirage. Her thin slippers caught on the pebbles under her feet, making her stumble.

At last she tumbled out of the cold, damp darkness of the cave into the night. She found herself on a narrow pathway high above the sea. Below, she could see the house, still lit up for the party, bobbing lights in the hills in the distance. She heard a shout, an echo, as if someone was calling a name. Her name?

In a burst of hope, she started to run down the winding path, uncaring of her aching feet. 'I'm here!' she shouted.

Until suddenly her path was blocked by a large, solid shadow stepping in front of her on the path. Luis.

He gave her a terrible smile, a ghost of the smiling grin he had used so often. Mary felt her heart lurch with panic. She backed up, pebbles tumbling down the path towards the sea.

'I am afraid I can't let you go quite so soon, my dear Senhorita Manning,' he said brightly.

Mary tried to back away further, but she found herself backed into a stand of coconut trees. She dared not take her attention from his face, from any waver that might warn her he was going to hit her again.

'I don't know what you hope to accomplish

by keeping me here,' she said, trying to stay calm. His eyes were so very cold, so flat; she knew he was seized by his cause and did not care who he hurt now. 'You will be followed here and I can't help you any more. I have no power in this quarrel, I barely even know the Braganzas and care nothing for their quarrels.'

'But your father does,' Luis said, still so calm. 'As does your admirer Lord Sebastian. His family has long been involved in Portuguese dealings, where they have no business. He has been rather a nuisance ever since he took over his brother's place in the English delegation. Lord Henry Barrett was so much more—amenable to other viewpoints.'

Mary was aghast. Lord Henry, Sebastian's brother, who had once been talked of as a possible suitor for *her*, had been well known for his promising future career in diplomacy. Was he a spy of sorts? 'What do you mean?'

'They said he would soon be posted to Portugal and he was more interested in feathering his own nest as well as helping us. It was most disappointing when he died. Lord Sebastian has made things much more difficult.'

'Then what is it you want Lord Sebastian to hear so very much?' she demanded. She slid around deliberately so he watched her and did not see the approaching lights.

Luis frowned. His handsome face was so distorted, he looked like an entirely different person. 'I will do anything to return to my home! You English—you are only after your own ends, Portugal means nothing to you.'

'You will do anything—even bully your own sister? Kidnap an innocent woman?'

'You are hardly an innocent, Senhorita Manning. You are the daughter of Sir William Manning, one of the architects of this removal to Brazil. You must know more than you would like to pretend.' She glimpsed a kindling of anger deep in his eyes, a flicker of light.

She saw the lanterns moving closer up the hill, heard a shout. Time was running out. She suddenly shoved Luis, hoping to catch him by surprise. He stumbled back and Mary took off running as fast as she could.

'I am here! Help!' she screamed.

But she did not get far. He regained his balance and caught up with her quickly. He grabbed her hard around her waist, swinging her off her feet. Mary screamed again, twisting around to claw at him, pull his hair. Anything to get away.

'Puta!' he shouted. He dropped her hard on to the path.

For an instant, all the breath was pushed from her body. She rolled away, ignoring the pain of the pebbles under her thin gown. She saw him grabbing for her and screamed again.

Suddenly, he was gone. She pushed herself up and saw through a blurry haze that Sebastian had found her at last. His face was a mask of fury in the moonlight, as he hauled Luis off her and hit him in the face. The two of them were a mere blur as they fought their way across the pathway, Luis slamming Sebastian into a tree only to be shoved away.

Mary scrambled to her feet, glancing around desperately for a weapon of her own, something to bash Luis over the head with, but there was nothing. Only boulders too large for her to grasp. She peered over the edge of the pathway, praying the lights were closer. 'Help!'

But there was no one close enough to hear

them. There was only the smell of blood and sweat heavy in the warm air, the sound of shouts. She pressed herself close to the boulder, staring in growing horror at the scene before her.

'I will never let you hurt another woman,' Sebastian said roughly, out of breath, as he pinned Luis's arm behind his back, driving him to the ground. 'Never come near Mary again!'

'She is not important, she never was,' Luis said with a terrible laugh. 'Nor was my sister. Women are never important, they never see—you are a man, you must know. If she had died, I would have been happy!' His free hand suddenly shot out and grabbed a rock. As he swung it up towards Sebastian's head, Mary screamed, terrified.

Sebastian ducked and the weight of his body made Luis fall forward. There was a sickening crunch and for an instant she couldn't see what had happened. Then Sebastian staggered to his feet and Luis was crumpled on the ground.

Sebastian straightened away from Luis's body, his face streaked with dust and blood in the faint light. He stepped towards her, his hand held out.

'Darling Mary—are you hurt?' he said, his voice rough.

Mary sobbed as she took a stumbling step towards him, hardly daring to believe he was real, that she was safe.

Before she could touch him, to hold on to him and know he was really there, Luis rose up with a great roar, like a demon night creature. He lunged towards them, a blade raised high against Sebastian's back. Startled, Sebastian ducked to one side, pushing Mary out of the way. Luis tumbled past him, falling into the darkness below the pathway with a horrible shout that echoed into silence.

Mary choked on a sob. She ran into Sebastian's arms, hiding her tear-streaked face against his shoulder. She held on to him tightly, fearing he would vanish in an instant. That this silence, this peace, was false.

'You found me,' she said, holding on to him as if he was a beautiful dream, sure to slip away into the strange nightmare that had been this night. All foolish arguments seemed like nothing; the past was gone. All that mattered was *now*, that he was there with her.

'I found you, my darling,' he whispered against her hair, holding her close. 'I was so afraid I would lose you all over again.'

'You could never lose me, Sebastian, not now.' Mary held on to him. She suddenly felt so weak, so exhausted. She shivered and Sebastian quickly removed his coat and wrapped it close around her. It was wonderfully warm, smelling of *him*, and he seemed to be all around her, keeping her safe.

The shouts seemed closer, the swaying lights in the night glowing like stars. 'We are here,' Sebastian called back. He wrapped his arms around Mary, helping her down the pathway. 'Don't look back, my dearest,' he whispered.

She did not look as he led her past Luis's crumpled body and yet it was all still there in her mind. The terrible fear of being alone in the darkness. The coppery smell of blood and fear. And the knowledge of her own strength, which she did not even realise she possessed before.

Would she ever be free of it again?

* * *

Sebastian cradled Mary close in his arms as he carried her along the shore path. She had fallen into an exhausted sleep, her head heavy on his shoulder. She was alive, safe. But his heart was far from at peace. She had been led to that terrible place because of *him*, because of all the secrets that had lain between them for too long.

There would be no more secrets, ever.

Mary was surely the bravest person he had ever known. She stood up for her family and friends, facing danger with a stout heart, and he loved her more every time he saw her. Loved her in a way he had never thought possible. She brought a light to his life he'd never had and his heart was full with her. With her smiles and laughter. Those had come far too close to being extinguished tonight.

He kissed her forehead gently and she sighed and shifted in his arms. She looked like an angel in the moonlight, *his* angel. He could not put her in danger any longer.

'No more secrets, my darling,' he whispered. 'That I promise you.'

Chapter Twenty-Three

Sebastian paced the corridor outside Sir William Manning's library, his hat in his hand, far more nervous than he had ever been before a battle, or even before beginning his diplomatic work. He was going to ask Sir William for his daughter's hand in marriage—and he could only pray the man would say yes.

It seemed like the most monumental moment in his life.

The door opened and one of Sir William's young secretaries came out. 'You may come in now, Lord Sebastian,' he said, before hurrying away with an armload of papers.

Sebastian took a deep breath and stepped into the room. He had been there before, of course, for his work, and it looked no different. A desk piled with papers and books, the window open to catch a warm breeze from the plaza outside. Sir William rose from his seat and held out his hand.

'Lord Sebastian,' he said with a small half-smile. 'I believe I can hazard a guess why you are here today.'

Sebastian had learned a great deal about how to read people since he had taken up a diplomatic career, but he feared he could not quite read Sir William's smile. Was it of welcome? Or would he toss him out on his ear? Sebastian could not quite blame him if he did. He knew he had to prove himself worthy of Mary now.

'I have made no secret of my tender feelings for your daughter, Sir William,' he said. 'I have indeed come to ask for your permission for us to marry.'

Sir William waved him to a chair. 'You have certainly been of much service to her, to us both, lately, and I am most grateful. But have you asked Mary this herself?'

'I have,' Sebastian said. 'And she has agreed.'

'As I am sure she would.' Sir William

reached for a small box on his desk and turned it over between his fingers, not quite looking at Sebastian. 'I love my daughter very much. She is all I have left of her mother. I have long hoped she would find someone she loves and who loves her back as much as she deserves. Are you that man?'

Sebastian nodded. He knew that now he was able to, had to, reveal his heart, to the whole world and not just to Mary. Everyone had to know how wonderful she was. 'I have known no true happiness, no true goodness, until I met Mary, Sir William. She is beautiful, of course, but also brave and honest. I know we will be able to work together for our family, for our country, and will love each other for the rest of our lives. I cannot do my work without her. And if you will give me the chance, I will prove to you how I can make her happy in return.'

Sir William slowly nodded. 'I have hoped that she would find someone like you. It is hard for me to let her go, but I can do it if I know she will be loved.'

'So she will be. Always.'

'I can see now that you mean that. And that you are the man for her, in a way your late brother could never have been.' Sir William opened the box and held it out to Sebastian.

Sebastian saw it was a miniature portrait, inlaid in a velvet lining. A woman with Mary's fair oval face and glossy dark hair smiled up at him, but her eyes were brown. Next to the image was a ring, a ruby set in pearls. 'That is Lady Manning?'

William smiled down at the painted image. 'So it is. Mary is much like her, as I am sure you can see, and not just in her prettiness. Maria was also brave, sometimes to the point I feared for her safety, and she was loyal and good. I was lucky to have her for as long as I did and now I can give you the gift she left me—our daughter. Perhaps you would like to give Mary her mother's ring as well? I know the Barretts must have jewels, but I know Maria would have liked that very much.'

Sebastian swallowed past the sudden knot in his throat. For so long in his life, he had longed for a family who would accept him and let him truly be a part of them, who he could work for and love. Had he now found that? He dared hope he had and it was yet another gift Mary had given him, just by being herself.

He felt like the most fortunate man in the world.

Sebastian reached for the ring and cradled it on his palm. It would indeed look lovely on Mary's finger. 'Thank you, Sir William. I know you are giving me the greatest gift ever and from the bottom of my heart I must thank you.'

Chapter Twenty-Four

Mary watched in the dressing table mirror as Adriana put the finishing touches on her *coiffure*, winding a wreath of white rosebuds through the elaborate curls to hold Mary's mother's lace mantilla in place.

'You have quite outdone yourself, Adriana,' Mary said with a happy laugh.

'Of course, *senhorita*. It is your wedding day! And you are the loveliest bride.'

Her wedding day. Mary could not stop smiling at those wondrous words. It was the day she had once thought could never be—the day she married Sebastian.

Outside her window, the sun was high in the clear azure sky, and the squares and lanes of Rio were quiet. Doña Carlota, her latest scheme foiled, had retired to her new villa in the hills with some of her courtiers and Dom Joao spent his days in his library, politics finally settled for the moment. The dinners and teas in honour of Mary's engagement had been nothing but merry. The only thing she did not like was that she and Sebastian had been too busy to do more than snatch a secret kiss or two.

And now the wedding was upon her and they would have long days just to themselves.

'There, I am all finished, *senhorita*,' Adriana said, affixing the last pearl-headed pin to Mary's *coiffure*. 'What do you think?'

Mary stood up to spin around before the mirror. Her gown, made by the same dressmaker who had created her masquerade costume, spun around her like a cloud, all pale-blue silk sewn with tiny pearls and crystals that sparkled in the light. Sebastian's gift to her, a pearl necklace with a clasp of Brazilian diamonds, shimmered around her throat and her hair gleamed a glossy darkness under the lace of her veil. Adriana had truly wrought miracles of stylishness that day.

'May I come in?' Teresa called from the doorway. Mary spun to a stop to see her friend standing there, a bouquet of tropical orchids in her hands and a rather hesitant smile on her lips. They had renewed their friendship since Luis's demise, but the traces of that terrible night still haunted Teresa's smile. Her face was rather pale, her eyes shadowed, despite the loveliness of her new burgundy pelisse and bonnet, but Mary had hopes that soon her friend would see a wedding of her own. Nicholas Warren had escorted Teresa to many parties of late.

'How lovely you look, Teresa,' Mary cried, and hurried over to take her bouquet. 'You will quite overshadow me.'

Teresa laughed. 'No one could do that. Surely Rio has never seen such a beautiful bride!'

'No, indeed,' Mary's father said as he hurried into the chamber, his watch in his hand as if he feared they would be late to the church. 'My dearest Mary. You are the very image of your mother. You have her beautiful eyes and also her kind heart and loyal soul. How she would have loved to see you today! She would be so happy, as I am, that you have found a love like ours was.'

'I wish she was here, as well.' Mary feared she would start to cry at his words, but she made herself laugh instead. She kissed her father's cheek, and took his outstretched hand. 'Shall we go, then?'

'Oh, yes,' he answered. 'Mustn't keep the vicar waiting…'

The English church, low and stolid, built of grey stone on a hillside, was not as grand as the cathedral, but it was full with every Englishman in Rio as Sir William led Mary through the open doors and into the vestibule. Teresa straightened her lacy train before taking her place in the front pew beside Mr Warren. The organ swelled with a glorious processional and Mary's hand tightened on her father's sleeve as he led her on to the blue carpet of the aisle.

For an instant, she could not breathe with the wondrous dreamlike feeling of the moment. Light streamed through the red and blue of the stained-glass windows, and brilliant tropical flowers were banked along the walls, sending their sweet scent into the air. But Mary could see nothing but Sebastian, waiting for her at the altar.

He was surely the most handsome man in the world, she thought, in his fine blue coat and white-satin waistcoat, his smile brilliant as he watched her move slowly towards him. Against the expected ceremony, he met her halfway down the aisle, catching her free hand in his. 'Mary,' he whispered. '*My* Mary, at last…'

'And my Sebastian,' she answered.

He laughed, and kissed her again. 'Always.'

Epilogue

The first Christmas of the Barrett family

'Do you see it, Maria?' Mary whispered. She gently waved the new crystal ornament, tied with a red bow for the baby's first Christmas, and let it catch the rays of bright golden sunlight that danced around the edges of the terrace. She laughed in delight as Maria reached for it with her chubby, pink hand.

Mary kissed those tiny fingers, marvelling at their perfection. Maria laughed, kicking out her feet under the hem of her muslin gown. Behind them, through the tall open doors of the terrace, their villa's drawing room was decorated with red, green and gold ribbons for the holiday, wound around gilt picture frames and brightening the pale colours of paint and up-holstery that kept the house so cool. Green wreaths made from palm leaves and tropical flowers hung over the doorways.

Like the improvised wreaths, that Christmas was unlike any Mary had ever known. Their new home, the low, white villa on the side of a hill where it could catch the sea breezes, was finally finished and her family living within its walls. Her father napped now in the shade, much more rested since Sebastian had inherited much of his work, and Maria's nursery was filled with dolls and rocking horses and tiny tea sets for her first Christmas presents.

Only a week ago, Mary had gone on Sebastian's arm to Teresa's wedding to Nicholas Warren, in the same church where she herself had been married and Maria christened. Mary had never thought Brazil, so exotic, so beautiful, so different from London, could be a true home, but now it was. More than she ever could have imagined.

'You know it is Christmas, don't you, my darling?' Mary whispered, swinging the crystal back and forth in front of her daughter's gaze. The baby's eyes were jewel-green, like her father's, and a fluff of dark hair crowned her perfect head. Mary was sure she would grow up to be a great beauty, and a most determined one, who would firmly grasp whatever she wanted, just as she did now with her crystal.

'It was only about a year ago that I found your father again—and realised how very wrong I had been about him,' Mary said, thinking of how very much life had changed. 'And now this year I have *you* and our new home. Christmas is a lovely time of year, no matter where we are!'

'I agree to *that*, most assuredly,' Sebastian said as he stepped on to the terrace. He still wore his riding boots, from the short journey from his work in Rio to their home. His new duties suited him, for he seemed most invigorated by their new life, just as Mary was. His skin glowed a pale gold from the touch of the sun and his hair was brighter than ever. But the best part was his smile, which was easier, wider, quicker than ever before. 'There is no better day.'

Mary laughed and leaped up to kiss his cheek. He smelled of the flowery breeze outside, the warm sun, and he held her close. 'You are home at last! We missed you.'

'As I have you.' He kissed her cheek, softly, a lingering touch, before he knelt down to reach for the baby's hand. Her fingers curled tight around his as she laughed and cooed and kicked.

'How are my ladies this lovely afternoon?' he said. 'I hope you haven't started the holiday party without me.'

'Never!' Mary said. 'We have only just finished our decorating, and came out here so Grandpapa could have a rest. He would never close his eyes if Maria was anywhere near! She wants her grandfather's attention at all times, laughing and chattering away at him.'

'Everyone must pay attention to our lovely miss whenever she calls for it, of course.' Sebastian made a face at his daughter, who giggled and kicked even harder.

'Teresa and Nicholas will arrive later and hopefully there will be a proper Christmas pudding for our dinner. The cook has been trying it for days.'

'And of course there will be a good rum punch.'

Mary laughed as she remembered her chokingly strong drink from the royal picnic by the sea. 'Maybe not *quite* so powerful. But we shall have a lovely holiday with our best friends and family around us.'

'It will be the finest Christmas ever. You and Maria are the best gifts I could ever have wished for,' Sebastian said. He swept her into his arms for a long, sweet kiss, even though there were no mistletoe boughs near. Even after months of marriage, his kiss thrilled her to her very toes, warmer even than the tropical sun.

She held him close as their baby gave a delighted coo. 'Oh, my darling Sebastian. I am sure no one ever had a finer holiday gift than this one...'

* * * * *

Author Note

I don't know about where you are, but here it has been a long, cold, grey winter—and I *hate* winter! So I was very happy to escape into writing Mary and Sebastian's story in the warmth of Brazilian sun and beaches. Even though in 1808 it wasn't exactly a beach as we think of it—with bikinis and drinks with tiny umbrellas—I was desperate enough to get out of the snow I would take any beach!

I had heard of the story about the flight of the Portuguese court from Lisbon to their colony in Brazil, but not really the details. Most of my previous research for the Napoleonic Wars centred on Spain and Waterloo. A few years ago, I came across Patrick Wilcken's book *Empire Adrift: The Portuguese Court in*

Rio de Janeiro, 1808-1821, in a second-hand bookshop, and started reading right there in the aisle. What a fascinating tale! On November the twenty-ninth, 1807, just days ahead of the Napoleonic Army under General Junot, almost fifteen thousand people—figures vary—sailed away from Lisbon harbour, under the protection of the British Navy, bound for Brazil, a land almost none of them had ever seen and which would prove to be a completely different world from wintertime Portugal. The royal court wouldn't return to Lisbon until 1821.

It was a tumultuous, complicated story of the 'Mad Queen' Maria, her son, the Prince Regent Joao, and his Spanish wife, Doña Carlota—a cousin whom he'd married when she was ten years old: they proved to be a disastrous mismatch—British commercial relations with Portugal that needed to be preserved at all costs, a stormy, months-long voyage and a landing in a new, strange world. It was like reading an epic novel, but it was all real and I loved putting Mary and Sebastian right in the middle of it all!

If you'd like to know more about this period in history—and there is so much more to know!—these are some books I found very useful:

Patrick Wilcken, *Empire Adrift: The Portuguese Court in Rio de Janeiro, 1808-1821* (2004)

Maria Graham, *Journal of a Voyage to Brazil and Residence There, 1821-23* (1824)

Kirsten Schultz, *Tropical Versailles: Empire, Monarchy, and the Portuguese Royal Court in Rio de Janeiro, 1808-1821* (2001)

Kenneth Light, *The Saving of an Empire: The Journey of Portugal's Court and Capital to Brazil, 1808* (2009)

Laurentino Gomes, *1808: The Flight of the Emperor* (2007)

Sir Henry Chamberlain, *Views and Costumes of the City and Neighbourhood of Rio de Janeiro, Brazil, from Drawings taken by Lieutenant Chamberlain, Royal Artillery, During the Years of 1819 and 1820, with Descriptive Explanations* (1822)

Marcus Cheke, *Carlota Joaquina, Queen of Portugal* (1947)

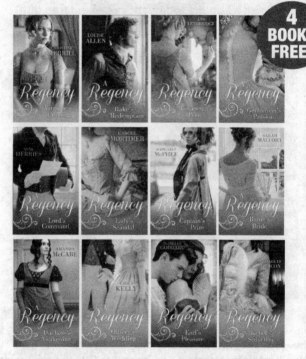

MILLS & BOON®

 HISTORICAL

AWAKEN THE ROMANCE OF THE PAST

sneak peek at next month's titles...

In stores from 4th December 2015:

His Christmas Countess – Louise Allen
The Captain's Christmas Bride – Annie Burrows
Lord Lansbury's Christmas Wedding
– Helen Dickson
Warrior of Fire – Michelle Willingham
Lady Rowena's Ruin – Carol Townend
Morrow Creek Marshal – Lisa Plumley

Available at WHSmith, Tesco, Asda, Eason, Amazon and Apple

Just can't wait?
Buy our books online a month before they hit the shops!
visit www.millsandboon.co.uk

These books are also available in eBook format!